BUT MY LUNCH

PATRICK FORSYTH
A COLLECTION OF SHORT STORIES

Copyright © Patrick Forsyth 2023

Without limiting the rights under copyright reserved above, no part of this publication may be reproduced, stored in, or introduced into a retrieval system, or transmitted in any form or by any means (electronic, mechanical, photocopying, recording or otherwise) without prior written permission of the copyright owner. The right of Patrick Forsyth to be identified as author of this work has been asserted in accordance with sections 77 and 78 of the Copyright, Designs and Patents Act, 1988. This book is a work of fiction. Names, characters, businesses, organisations, places, and events are either the product of the author's imagination or are used fictionally. Any resemblance to actual persons, living or dead, events or locales is entirely coincidental.

This edition Published by Touchstone:tc (Maldon).
ISBN: 9798862007558

The author may be contacted via
www.patrickforsyth.com

This is dedicated to Teesa Proudfoot: as nice a sister as one could wish for, even if she regularly reminds me that I am her "much older brother".

Q. How many mystery writers does it take to change a light bulb?

A. *One to take out the old and almost screw in the new. But a second is often needed to add a final twist.*

(I like this, though not all the stories here are mysteries!)

CONTENTS

Introduction — 1
Getting there — 5
Branching out — 7
The good the bad and the tongue tied — 13
Twice upon a time — 18
A good read — 22
Disappearing trick — 27
Brushing away the past — 36
A night to remember — 42
Who'd be a writer? — 47
The curious case of the lost umbrella — 53
Bus stop — 58
Radical Treatment — 62
Just a simple signature — 66
Are we nearly there? — 72
A rather unusual day — 77
Another day, another tour — 81
Gutted — 86
A bit of a shock — 92
Planned exit — 98
Fair Warning — 103
It takes two — 108
But not for lunch — 113
None like it hot — 118
Something of an obsession — 123
A meeting will sort it out — 127
Marking time — 131
Seasonal Health and safety — 136
Ding dong grumpily on high — 142
No blame — 147

A peaceful life — 151
A lucky encounter — 157
Holiday work — 163
Down the garden path — 167
A break by the beach — 172
The bucket list — 177
Sometimes only a letter will do — 181
An early morning proposal — 186
Are you sitting comfortably? — 190
Afterword — 195
Write right — 199
Other titles — 203

THE AUTHOR

Patrick Forsyth is best known for much non-fiction writing: with many how-to style books and articles published about business and career skills. He has also had three light-hearted books of travel writing published, all set in Southeast Asia: *First Class at Last!, Beguiling Burma* and *Smile because it happened* (the latter about the so-called land of smiles - Thailand).

He has also had five novels published: the latest is *Where there's a will* about which one reviewer said:

"Once again Patrick brings a mixture of intrigue and plot twisting while creating characters you might meet down the coffee shop."
Tony Fisher, BBC broadcaster and writer

Details of these titles appear on page 203.

Patrick lives in Maldon, in Southeast England, and writes looking out at the estuary of the River Blackwater.

Introduction

"What no wife of a writer can ever understand is that a writer is working when he's staring out of the window."
Burton Rascoe

Most writers (of whatever gender) will identify with the quotation above from American journalist Burton Roscoe; it infers that writing tends to be all consuming. Certainly, it is easy to become obsessive about it, but writing can also be satisfying and having a piece of any sort finished and made public is always a special moment. As indeed is having anything published.

The writer Stephen King once described books as portable magic and many would regard this description as most apt for fiction. I have had five novels published (see page 200), but the first fiction I wrote, which saw me initially, and tentatively, branching away from non-fiction and business writing, was in the form of short stories. Such supplied steppingstones to my writing my first complete novel; indeed, the classic short story form has an addictive quality for many writer; the length may be short, but each must contain all the elements of a complete story.

Over the last few years, the number of stories I have written has grown steadily, especially during the recent lockdowns, when writing kept me busy and sane. I am now pleased to see some of my favorite ones published in this volume. The tales here form an eclectic mix. Some are (I hope) funny, some sad, many have something of a twist in the tale; they are short stories designed to go well with a cuppa, or a brief read before settling down to sleep. Though those included in this book are all stand-alone I have added a brief comment to most just to put them in any necessary context.

A couple have been published in anthologies, and here I would mention one, *A Great Little Gallimaufry.* This is a title which I edited and organized the publication of to raise money for Farleigh Hospice. This is an organization based in Chelmsford in Essex, for which I am an Ambassador and which is regarded as an outstanding outfit worthy of support. That book contains writing by a group of writers from around the county. It is, I think, still available and Farleigh can be contacted via: www.farleighhospice.org should you want to buy a copy. Several of my stories published here have won, or won a place in, writing competitions, though sadly not in circumstances that resulted in their publication.

The first one here, reproduced within this Introduction, is what is called flash fiction, a term used to describe the very, very short story. Way back on the day I first attended a writing group, a competition in the *Daily Telegraph* was current. Entries had to be what they named "mini sagas" - that is complete stories consisting of exactly fifty words not counting the title, and members of the writing group were instructed by its then leader to follow the brief as an exercise. Subsequently several of us submitted our attempts to the newspaper and, surprise, surprise, mine was placed fourth (out of nearly three thousand entries); it was later published in a little book of what were regarded as the best, which was edited by Brian Aldiss. My prize was a place on a one-week residential writing course worth the best part of five hundred pounds no less. I think the thought of receiving ten pounds a word spurred me on even more than attending the course did! The story follows:

A dream so real

Staying overnight with friends, his sleep was interrupted by a vivid dream: a thief broke in, stole everything in the flat – then carefully replaced every single item with an exact replica.

"It felt so real," he told his friends in the morning.

Horrified, uncomprehending, they replied, "But who are you?"

My only gripe about this was that the book was divided into about a dozen story groupings with headings like Human Nature, Travelling and Love, while mine appeared in the last section which was headed, "Some Eccentricities." Really! That apart, the whole experience prompted me to write more.

Many of the stories reproduced here were written to fit the brief of the two writing groups to which I belong. There is usually a "theme" set for pieces to be read at meetings and also a maximum length (so that stories can be read out in a manageable time); though sometimes people link to the "theme" in a very contrived way. This not only because it makes it easier to think of something appropriate but also because the very act of contrivance can itself be fun.

I am aways grateful for the support and feedback I receive from group members... even when their critique may be negative! A big thank you to all concerned.

I rather feel that the pieces included in this book are about due to see the light of day and, appropriately I hope, I have made the first one chosen a short piece which is about a writer. I hope readers will enjoy all that is included here. So, as Joanna Lumley wrote in a Foreword to the *Daily Telegraph* Mini-Saga book – I wish you bon appetit.

Patrick Forsyth. Maldon, Essex.

Getting there

He pressed "Print" and watched the printer disgorge a page. He read it over, screwed it into a ball and threw it at the waste-paper basket in the corner. It missed, as had a dozen others; anyway, the bin was full. He returned to the keyboard and stared at it blankly as if it might do something on its own. It didn't. He stabbed half-heartedly at the keys, not quite randomly, that would be silly, but with little enthusiasm.

This was ridiculous: all that was required was a short story. But just how much can be described in only 500 words? Not all that much. Certainly, there was no need for a long complex plot. Just a few minutes of action should do. He typed some more, printed again and then screwed up the sheet after reading only the first line: *It was a dark and stormy night...* what? No! Starting with a blatant cliché was hardly likely to go anywhere. It shouldn't be a problem; writers' block was usually cured by thinking of the mortgage, putting a note of the deadline on a yellow sticky reminder attached to the computer, or, at worst, by a quick burst of plagiarism. What was the old saying? *Plagiarism is stealing from one person; research is stealing from many.* So actually, what was needed was a quick burst of research. Einstein was once reputed to have said, *Of course I don't know what I'm doing, if I did know it wouldn't be called research.* He tossed another sheet across the room; he didn't know what he was doing right now, that was for sure.

He needed to select an appropriate 'genre', find a plot, some incidents, a beginning, middle and an end. Even settling on one thing would be a start. Let's make the main character a man, he thought, then there's the question of what sort of man: what's he doing, is there conflict, is there a problem, will the story see it overcome, will the end be happy, sad or enigmatic? The mood he was in it would most likely be sad. Maybe he could start with the end: a resolution, an enigma... something, anything. Then he could work backwards: not so much "Ready, aim, fire" as fire first and fill in the blanks afterwards. There's a thought: maybe there should be a gun involved, a crime, a murder. Maybe not, but a problem must certainly feature. Finally, he thought he had an idea, well sort of, anyway. He resumed typing.

If the main character was a writer, he thought, what could happen then? A deadline looming, his imagination flagging, despair pervading all; but then a resolution would be necessary to create an ending. Think, think ... wait a minute; he pressed more keys. Now he had something. He typed on, purposefully now, seeing the shape of it at last. He was very near the end. He glanced down at the corner of his computer screen. It read "500 words". Exactly right. Phew! Done. The end.

"Getting there" is a short piece, chosen because it is about the writing process and thus sets the scene for what is to follow here. Someone, I forget who, defined a writer as being someone for whom writing is more difficult than for other people. This piece reflects that: I would hate people to think that writing is too easy, even while hoping it is never as difficult as described here.

Branching out

The ground looked a long way down and Chloe now felt that she had climbed too high. Her friend Milly had been sure, she had egged her on, she had reassured her it would be fine.

"Go on, you can reach... put your right foot there... stretch, stretch... yes, you can do it... the view will be great."

It was a great view, but it was, well, it was high. Too high. Chloe called down to Milly, "I'm up", but she also bit her lip and tried to stop a tear she felt appearing in her eye. There could be no doubt that she had gone too high. A gust of wind blew across the garden and the leaves around her in the tree rustled, Chloe found the noise a little scary, but she struggled to turn round and managed to move her left foot to a lower branch. Could she get down or was she stuck? Where was Milly? She had been shouting encouragement from the foot of the tree, encouragement and instructions, but now she appeared to have wandered off leaving Chloe stranded high up amongst the branches. She was not at all sure she could get down. She moved her right foot to a new position and was then perhaps just a foot lower.

What would happen if she couldn't get down? Chloe may only have been six years old, but she knew about the Fire Brigade being called to rescue cats from trees, she remembered reading about it in a book: *The great cat rescue.* Maybe they would have to come and rescue her, maybe Milly could go to the house and organise it. But she worried about what her Mum would say: she had been expressly told not to climb the tree, "It's dangerous," her mother had said, "you don't want to fall do you? You might hurt yourself." If Milly hadn't suggested the climb, she might never have done it. Milly was a year or so older than Chloe, she knew things and she said it would be fine. Where was she?

As she wondered where her friend had gone, her foot slipped and, losing her balance, she slipped down a couple of feet; she might have fallen clean out of the tree, but she grabbed on with her right hand and steered her wayward foot onto a secure branch. She found she was shaking a little and, looking down, saw that she had scuffed her new yellow shoes. The tear that had been threatening to appear now did so and, as it trickled down her cheek, she hung on and took a moment to make sure she was secure.

Milly was her best friend, and they did so much together. Any game was better if Milly was there and Chloe trusted her, she often had good ideas and she had said it would be okay to make the climb. After remaining still for a few moments, Chloe felt steadier and, moving carefully, she came down a few more feet. But she was not retracing her steps, she was on a new route, and she was now, well, she was sort of stuck. She called out, "I'm stuck, Milly, can you show me where to go next?" Silence. "Please, pretty please," she added, but the silence continued; where had the silly girl gone, just when a friend was really needed.

Then she heard her mother call from the house: "Chloe!" And then again, "Chloeeee" – she extended the final 'e' as she shouted. "Lunch time." Chloe knew she should go to the house, she struggled to get down, she was just too high to jump the last bit but, although she got a foot or two lower, she also got more stuck. She could hear her mother calling again, but she didn't want to admit she was stuck; having been told she was not to climb the tree, she might be in trouble having done so. She made no reply and clung there for what seemed like an age, until finally her mother walked down the garden and stood under the tree; she had known exactly where to look.

"Well, young lady, and what are you doing up there?" She said sternly.

Chloe sniffed and admitted, "I'm stuck," coupling it with her most sheepish look, her expressive, blue eyes seeking forgiveness.

"I seem to remember saying that you should *not* climb the tree, do you remember that?"

Chloe sniffed again. "Yes. But Milly said it would be fine, she helped me on the way up and it was only on the way down I got stuck. I thought you might need to call the Fire Brigade, like for a cat, would that cost a lot?" She tried to put a brave face on things, but her voice had a pleading tone to it.

"I don't think we need the Fire Brigade, let's see what we can do, shall we?" Said her mother looking up at her.

"Can you turn round a little, that's right, now stretch your right foot to the branch over there – just a little further down. See? Okay, good, you're a bit lower now and if you turn again and face me, I think you can jump and I'll catch you, okay?"

Chloe turned, relieved to see that she was now not so far from the ground and her Mum was holding out her arms. A moment later she got a big hug as well as a reprimand and she held her Mum's hand as they walked towards the house and the waiting lunch. Chloe looked back over her shoulder and saw Milly following some steps behind.

"You were no help," she called, "I could have been up there all day."

As Chloe sat at her place in the kitchen her mother posed her a question: "How old are you?"

"You know how old I..." Chloe stopped as she saw her mother give her a look that clearly said, 'answer the question', and she finished simply, "I'm six."

"That's right, you're six, and getting quite grown up now, aren't you?" She did not wait for an answer, continuing as she served up Chloe's lunch. "Now you *do know* that Milly isn't real, don't you?" Chloe's invisible friend had appeared when she was two and a half, she had become so ubiquitous that even Chloe's Mum sometimes thought of her as real. Certainly, she was a real presence in the household, even if a fictitious one.

"I suppose," said Chloe, "but she's sort of real, like people in books, they aren't real, I know that, but they are sort of real."

Chloe loved her books, and her mother used the fact to move on.

"Okay, but as you get older you leave some books behind, don't you? As you read better and better there are certain ones you put aside and different ones, better ones, with new characters replace them. Every week you go to the mobile library when it stops by the Post Office and ask that nice Mrs Brown for something new. Right?"

"Yes." Chloe nodded; she liked Mrs Brown, and her books.

"Well, I think it's time to regard Milly like a book you have grown out of, to put her on one side and move on, especially if she gets you stuck in trees. What do you think, can you do that?"

"I suppose." Chloe understood. She knew Milly wasn't real and she knew also that it was time. Only the other day she had said something about Milly to her friend Georgie and found she got a funny look in return.

And besides, she had been no help at all when she had to get down the tree. Right, she decided, time to move on.

"Okay," she said. "No more Milly, can I have another sausage?"

"Can I have another sausage, what?"

"Can I have another sausage, please?"

As her mother went to the cooker and Chloe tucked into her lunch with gusto, standing at the door to the garden Milly had heard everything they said. She well knew how it worked: all children grew out of their imaginary friends in time and Chloe was clearly at that stage. Milly turned and walked away, although she had been very happy with Chloe, she didn't look back. She had to find a new opening for herself: a new position in life, a new someone to link up with and she had to do so quickly. It was a matter of life and death. She held her arm out in front of her as she walked, it seemed to her it was already beginning to look a little translucent; unless she found a new friend soon it would dim, and finally all of her would simply fade away.

She picked up her pace.

"Branching out" won a prize in a competition organised by The Society of Women Writers & Journalists (SWWJ), an excellent body of professional writers that meets regularly in London and of which I was recently elected a Fellow – yes, they do have men members too! To keep judging impartial, entries are identified only by a number, the names revealed only as results are announced. At one of their London functions those placed were called up in turn to collect a certificate from the lady judge, in a room predominantly full of women. As she opened the envelope and saw my name she exclaimed in surprise, "Oh, my goodness, it's a man!" When I got to the front it was not too difficult to say a few words after that. It is always good to have work

recognised by your peers, especially for this, a story that is not quite what it appears.

The good, the bad and the tongue-tied

It was so *very* much not his thing; Harry hated and feared it and just knew he was no good at it at all. He was sweating and his hands were shaking, but he was doing it; reluctantly, very reluctantly, but doing it nevertheless.

But then he had been given no option.

"Okay, I would be pleased to join the committee," he had said some months earlier. Christopher Morris was slightly intimidating. He was tall, with a military bearing and had a small moustache, neatly clipped, but dangerously reminiscent of Adolf Hitler. However, the local charity he chaired was certainly worthwhile and Harry really needed some such activity to keep him busy in retirement. Thus, he found himself joining a dozen other people from various walks of life, all nice enough and all united in their commitment to support the local charity.

Eager to fit in and to make a difference, Harry had gradually got more and more involved and took on various tasks as matters came up at the committee meetings.

"Yes, I'll get that printed."

"Right, I'll track that down; no problem."

It all kept him busy; he got on well with most of the others involved and, importantly, he felt that together they made a worthwhile difference. However, although he got things done, Christopher was a poor listener, and more than somewhat inclined to monopolise proceedings. These were not ideal characteristics for someone in the Chair. Harry was not alone in feeling that Christopher was in fact a bit of a bully, though rarely did anyone actually stand up to his 'when I want your opinion, I'll give it to you' school of chairmanship.

It was just as the last committee meeting finished that he had said to Harry:

"You know that talk we've been asked to give to that group next week?"

"Yes," Harry acknowledged that he did, wondering where this might be going. He had earlier agreed to attend the fundraiser together with a number of other committee members.

"Well, I've given them your name. I know you said you'd come to the meeting, and we need to increase the number of us that do the speaking at this sort of thing. Gives us more flexibility. So, over to you then."

Harry was appalled. Speak in public! No, no, no – it was his worst, his very worst nightmare. He had not expected being on the committee to involve *this*. He blanched at the thought. But even as he spluttered out a refusal, he saw that the other committee members had all left and Christopher dismissed his response with a snort, turned his back and made a rapid departure from the meeting room. Harry spent a miserable few days in part thinking of how he could get out of it and in part trying to think of how to go about doing it. He felt no great success in either case.

So, in due course, he found himself on a raised platform, with the best part of a hundred people in front of him. He *had* thought about it, of course he had, but his copious notes were not helping him one tiny bit. Somehow, he found he could hardly see the audience; they were just a blur. In his mind's eye he saw only a vision of his own figure, clutching the lectern in front of him sufficiently hard to turn his knuckles white, the hand holding his notes shaking and the fear rising visibly from him like a mist.

"Um. What I would like to say... err, what I mean to say is... Sorry, um, I don't think I am making that very clear." Harry knew he was dying a death. He felt a dire certainty that the audience hated him and that they would rather chew off their own fingers than listen to him for a single moment longer. But the cause was important. So, he struggled on, wishing the ground would open and swallow him up, his voice declining nearer to a mumble rather than sounding clearer. Then a voice from the back of the hall interrupted him.

"Sorry to interrupt, but I can't really hear you properly."

Harry's mind was in overdrive: how could Christopher have put him in this position, without even a vestige of consultation? He heard the voice at the back continuing:

"Please just speak up a bit. This is fascinating, it's such a good cause – I hope you are going to ask for donations. I am sure many of us here will want to help." The last sentence was spoken clearly and slowly.

"Yes, I am." Following the example of whoever had interrupted him, Harry managed a short sentence without hesitation. Then, spurred on by what had unexpectedly proved to be an encouraging comment, he gained some confidence, and the next bit went much better. Seeing people nodding in agreement his confidence grew further and he made progress through his notes. Suddenly he had an idea: he knew just how to finish. Furthermore, he knew he would enjoy putting over his last point and, after all, the whole point of the event was to raise money for the cause. He might have been unceremoniously thrown in at the deep end, but now he was learning fast. His voice was finally steady, from relief perhaps at approaching his chosen ending, and he spoke up loud and clear.

"One final thing. The gentleman who spoke from the back earlier was correct: I *am* going to ask for donations, that's what we are here for, so please be generous – please be *very* generous. It's such a good cause. As a start let me say this." He looked straight at his chairman, who sat smugly at the back of the room his arms folded; he pointed at him, willing his hand to remain steady.

"As you know Christopher Morris there chairs this charity, he deputed me to give this talk. And he told me earlier that he would lead the way, making a public donation to encourage others. A generous gesture, I am sure you will agree. Thank you, Christopher. I think £500 was the figure you mentioned, isn't that right?"

Harry fell silent. He didn't know quite what to say next… but he found he had discovered the dramatic pause. Seconds ticked by and every head in the room turned towards Christopher, and again Harry's anonymous interrupter spoke up.

"Well done, Christopher, I've a cheque here to match yours. So… a thousand pounds already, come on everybody!"

Christopher looked daggers at Harry, but he spoke out briefly, and uncharacteristically quietly: "Yes, five hundred pounds from me." What else could he say?

Harry managed a closing remark and finally sat down to considerable applause; donations continued to be made and later he found he had helped raise a considerable sum of money for the charity. Maybe, he thought, this public speaking business was something he could do after all; certainly, one of his final phrases had, he felt, come out exactly right.

"Thank you, Christopher," he had said, "though I must say you seemed to find your donation as unexpected as it was for me to find myself put on the spot today and up here on this platform."

"The good, the bad and the tongue-tied" is a story that I can identify with in two ways. I have sat on a fair number of committees over the years and know the need to "persuade" people to assist in various ways if everything is going to get done, not least when raising money for a charity is concerned. I have also done a good deal of public speaking with my business hat on, and, in recent years, I have given talks about my writing to the likes of u3a [University of the Third Age], Women's Institutes, Rotary Clubs and the like. It can be a somewhat traumatic event, especially for the unprepared. I also have a talk I give with the title, "The good, the bad and the tongue-tied", about the art of speaking in public, how to go about it and the funny things that sometimes happen on such occasions.

Twice upon a time

Becky couldn't sleep. She lay awake, her mind buzzing. She knew it was late and that she should not be awake, and she didn't want to spoil a day of the holidays by being tired all the next day. She closed her eyes, but she still didn't fall asleep. When she opened her eyes again there was someone looking at her; a very little someone. Sitting crossed legged on her bedside table between the book she had been reading before the light went out and her clock was a tiny figure: it was, unmistakeably, a fairy. She had gossamer wings, a frilly, white dress and long blond hair. She reached up to brush her hair away from her eyes before saying simply.

"Hello. Can't you sleep?" For some reason this did not strike Becky as peculiar, and she just answered: "No."

"Maybe I can help. I could grant you a wish," said the fairy.

"Really, wow, that's wonderful," said Becky, her mind instantly full of things she would like.

"Just a small wish, just enough to get you happily to sleep, then I must go; it must all be done before midnight."

Becky didn't pause to think how odd all this was, excited she just launched into suggestions.

"I would like more curly hair, more pocket money, and more shoes and Lego," she exclaimed eagerly. "Can I wish for that?" The fairy looked uncertain, and for a second she said nothing, allowing Becky to rush on:

"And I'd like more time to play on my tablet. Yes, more, more, more," she said, her mind racing as she went on: "...and more..." But the fairy interrupted her.

"That is rather a lot," she said. "One might even say it's a bit greedy."

"But I want it all," said Becky, her voice sounding strident.

"Well, I'm afraid it's too much, but maybe I can give you just one more."

"One more *what?* That doesn't seem very... well, I'm not sure what you mean."

"You'll see."

The fairy smiled, then clicked her fingers and a small flash of light sprang from her hand, flitted between them and buffeted Becky's cheek. For an instant as it touched her it felt like cotton wool.

Becky didn't think this boded too well and though she didn't want to sound ungrateful, she wanted to know exactly what the fairy meant by "one more". So, she planned to say, "*Before I say anything else, please tell me - more what?*" But what she said came out weird:

"<u>Befive</u> I say anything else..." She didn't finish the sentence, thinking that couldn't be right. She tried again: "<u>Befive</u> I say..." Then she realised it was one more, one more than... <u>befive?</u> She couldn't even_*think* the right word. It was actually just as the fairy had promised. She tried again:

"I can see what you've done, but how is that going <u>three</u> help me? I don't think it will make it easier five me three get three sleep," she said. Again, she found she'd added one and what she'd said was not quite what she meant, but her voice seemed to have a mind of its own.

"You did ask for so much more and I thought just one more might teach you a lesson," came the reply.

"Well, yes, but not this. I thought wishes would be

twoderful, but that's not so. I thought threenight was my two and only chance of a wish coming true, but in fact threenight's just an unfortun-nine disaster. Urrgh!" She spluttered, her words just wouldn't come out right, but she struggled on.

"I hate you; you are a threefaced triple crosser. At least this is only until midnight when the clock strikes thirteen it will stop, right? It *will* stop then, won't it?"

"Yes, of course."

Suddenly Becky's Mother's voice came up the stairs.

"Go to sleep you. I can hear you chattering." Becky shouted something back, but quickly turned again to the fairy.

"All this is giving me a headache, I just wanted to make some wishes, I didn't fivesee all this. My fivehead hurts, right behind my three eyes, oh please make it stop. Please."

"It will be midnight very soon, just go back to sleep and everything will be back to normal in the morning, then maybe tomorrow night if I come again, then you can find a single simple wish for me to grant."

Becky lay back on her pillow and closed her eyes. She kept them shut for what seemed like a very long time until she heard the clock in the hall downstairs start to strike midnight. She started to count the chimes and opened her eyes as she did so, but the room was empty, the tiny fairy had vanished. She closed them again and continued counting. She found she could wonder if the chiming would stop at twelve or thirteen, but at number ten she fell asleep.

In the morning at breakfast while she ate a piece of toast, her mother asked her how she was.

"You were awake rather late last night, I think," she said. Becky thought for a moment and decided not to mention the visit of the tiny fairy. She wondered if she would see her again.

"Well?" Her mother pursued the point, adding, "and what would you like to do today?"

"I'm fine, but I'm not sure what to do," replied Becky after a moment, "but I am going to be very, *very* careful what I wish for!"

"Twice upon a time" is a short piece I submitted to a competition for a fairy story.; it did not win but was placed fourth and labelled 'Highly Commended.'

A good read

Jeramiah "Jerry" Johnson looked terrible. His face had a grey ghostly pallor, his hair hung in greasy clumps almost to his shoulders, and he looked thin and emaciated almost to the point where it seemed a stiff breeze might blow him over. He shuffled rather than walked across the room towards where his friend Arnold sat in a high-backed chair with a crumpled newspaper on his lap watching him approach.

"I feel like death," said Jerry. "What an earth did you have us drinking last night?" His friend sighed, after so long imprisoned together he was well used to Jerry's moods, moroseness and his tendency to acquire hangovers as thick as estuary mud.

"All down to you that, I can't touch the stuff. Anyway, has it not crossed your mind that your feeling like death is a natural consequence," he responded, shuffling the newspaper in his lap and folding it open at a particular page.

Jerry seemed determined to be especially surly that morning, he let out a long sigh turning it at the end into a comment:

"What do you mean consequence?" He asked as he slowly pulled up another chair and lowered himself into it.

"Well, just think about it, your feeling-like-death demeanour is surely only for the very good reason that you are, in fact, dead. They gave you a certificate for goodness sake," said Arnold, in a matter of fact tone that matched the logic of the point he'd just made.

"Yeah, right, but just because I'm dead shouldn't mean I have to feel this awful, I died of a stroke in a moment, I wasn't sick."

"So, you were fine apart from the blood clot you mean?" Arnold tried to inject a sympathetic tone into his comment, but Jerry didn't see that or the irony. "Anyway, you're feeling rough because you had *too many spirits* last night, it's not a left over from your untimely death you know." He paused wondered whether to make the 'too many spirits' comment again as it had made no impression on Jerry at all. He decided that some attempts at ghostly humour were destined to fall on stony ground and moved on.

"Come on," he continued, "I really have a good plan here, you could help me sort out the details."

The newspaper was open at a page headed *Armed robber on the run* and had Arnold's photo on it. It charted his criminal career from shop lifting at fourteen, through criminal damage, burglary, arson and grievous bodily harm; then finally to armed robbery.

"You do know there's a fatal flaw in your plan, don't you?" said Jerry.

"Come on," came the reply, "can there be a *fatal* flaw in a dead man's plan? Anyway, it's fool proof."

"Not so, just listen, you know that neither of us understands why we are still here on earth and how all this works. I mean, here we are sitting on these chairs, and my goodness I'm grateful to be sitting down the state I'm in after last night, and we can feel the chairs, can't we?" He did not wait for an answer to what was clearly a rhetorical question, and went on: "But that's not the case about everything is it?" He stuck out his arm just as the assistant librarian walked by and he walked through it as if it were mist.

"See. He can't hear us either can he? Here we are sitting right in the middle of the damn library, staff and library members moving about here all day and no one knows anything about us."

"Well yes, but there are some things that we can feel, right." He rustled the newspaper as he spoke. "I mean you poured your whisky okay last night didn't you, more than once, and it went down okay too."

"Yeah, but I don't know how, and I don't know where it went either for that matter, I haven't pissed for fifty-three years. Like I said we don't know how any of this works."

"Well, I'm pretty sure I know why I'm here in the library," said Arnold, "this is where I was cornered after the bank job. When they thought I was going to shoot that policeman, they gunned me down. I never would have; my gun was a fake, but I've been stuck here ever since. I wasn't a great reader before that, but here for all this time I have read practically every damn book in the place, even the Mills & Boon – and no I don't know why I can turn the pages – but without reading I would have gone raving mad. I'm glad you had your stroke here, it's been nice to have company, even if you are a morose old bugger – and if you tell that story about the elderly couple and the rice pudding again I think we'll find out if you can die twice because I shall certainly kill you."

"Well *thank you*, here I am saving you from terminal boredom – well post-terminal boredom maybe – and you want to do away with me, it's..."

Arnold interrupted him: "I'm just saying, anyway you're even more important to me now, with all the budget cuts the library is having, no new books are coming in. I'll either have to start re-reading some books or read the Jeffery Archer titles I skipped them on the first round. If my plan works I..."

"It won't work, it really won't. It's ridiculous. You

can't turn yourself in for the reward. Think about it. You're dead, the offer of a reward will have ceased long ago, presumably, well, when you ceased. Besides, you can't touch money and what would you spend it on if you could? Something else you can't touch? We can't leave the library and the only things they sell here are battered books and charity Christmas cards – you've read all the books and you've no one to send cards to. It's not a plan, it's not even the beginnings of a plan – it's a veritable parcel of contradictions."

"Well, all right, perhaps it was a little over optimistic. But we must do something, we have to get out of here, otherwise I for one will surely be raving mad as well as dead." Arnold looked resigned. He slowly closed the newspaper covering a sub heading reading, *Reward for capture.*

"I'm sorry, but I'm stuck here too remember. There must be a way, there must be a simple solution. Just keep thinking." They lapsed into silence and quietly the library continued about its business oblivious to their presence.

Another year went by, with no solution coming to them, then one day, one day seemingly no different from the now many days that had gone before, the library around them suddenly started to fade. Everything got less distinct and finally it faded away completely; as it did so it was replaced by a blinding brightness and eventually Jerry got to ask why they had been stuck in the library for so many years. The answer proved to be simple: "I shouldn't really tell you about Arnold," he was told, "client confidentiality – but you were stuck with him as you both died in the library at the same time. It's just how it is, people may stay in limbo until sufficient penance has been done."

"And my penance was fifty-eight years trapped in a

library?" He queried. "No," he was told, "it was just until Arnold had read the last of the novels by Jeffrey Archer."

I am sure this is most unfair to someone who is, after all, a very successful writer, but whose writing, for whatever reason, also carries the reputation of being, what shall I say, lowbrow.

Disappearing trick

He sometimes thought it had been a mistake. Although he claimed to be innocent, Bernie "Breakout" Bellingham had been in prison for four long years. It was early morning and the shout of one of the wardens echoed along the corridor.

"Come on, hurry along you horrible lot, or don't you want any breakfast?"

Bernie and his cellmate, Don "Driver" Desmond, made their way to the dining hall following what was a predictable daily routine. But today was different, at least in one respect and at least for Bernie.

"Sit down and listen up, Breakout, you and I have shared a prison cell for best part of four whole years now and I know it's your anniversary today – but you're still here. Much longer and your credibility will be rock bottom!" It was an annual joke and Don chuckled as he said it. Bernie raised an eyebrow and gave a knowing smile.

The clatter of metal trays around them and the chatter of fellow prisoners too made conversation difficult; Bernie was silent for a moment as he washed a mouthful of toast down with his tea. He had certainly said he would escape, though that was just in a perhaps mistaken fit of bravado when he had first arrived in prison. Incarceration was a dreary business, only made less grey by his imagination. His stories of dressing up as a warden or leaving hidden in a rubbish bin were treated with derision, but then prompted a good deal of mostly good-natured banter. A somewhat chunky forty-year-old he could never be mistaken for a potential escapee, and he knew in his heart that the chances of his making an escape were about as likely as getting piping hot pizza delivered to his cell. Besides, he thought, where would he go if he did get out? All he really wanted to do was go home. Finally, he answered.

"Yeah, right, perhaps it was a mistake to have said I'd break out when I first arrived here. Immediately got me my nickname, didn't it Don. I can't remember the last time anyone here called me Bernie. There's still time though, I have more of my sentence to go remember. You wait, right? You know how daunting it is when you first arrive here, maybe I should never have said I'd escape, but it's made for some fun along the way hasn't it?

"Suppose so, it's dreary enough in here, and I guess your tales of planned escapes have been a bit of a diversion – we all remember the way you described dressing up as a warden to walk out at the end of a shift. Not really credible though was it, you're no Steve McQueen now, are you? You're about as likely to escape from here as I am to organise beer on tap in our cell." An image of *The Great Escape* actor formed in Bernie's mind, and he had to agree.

"Okay, okay, I get out of breath getting into the top bunk and I suppose my escaping is a bit, well, unlikely. Besides what would I do if I got out? Can you see me on the run? I can't dance the tango and don't fancy eating guinea pig, so exile in South America ain't a very appealing prospect. Anyway, my wife's stood by me, you know Mary visits regularly, and I can't wait to get out and be back home. But you never know, do you. Maybe I will escape." Bernie paused, before continuing. "It's not impossible, Don. I told you, there's still some time to go, so you just watch this space! I've got a new plan now that

I'm working in the library: it involves disguising myself as an encyclopaedia and getting out in the van that delivers books to the library!"

"Oh, for goodness sake, come on! Breakfast's over, we need to move out of here."

"Yeah, okay, I'm coming, my shift in the library starts soon."

As the meal finished and they made their way out, several other prisoners called out to him.

"A whole year gone and you're still here, Breakout."

"This your last prison breakfast, Breakout? Don't forget to say 'Goodbye' before you go." Bernie just smiled.

"Everyone knows, don't they, Don? I may well have to actually do something, come up with a real plan. I'll give it some thought. You'll see!"

Lying on his bunk that night Bernie thought on the matter. It was not something he normally bothered about, maybe he was dwelling on it now only because today he had been inside exactly four years but maybe, he thought suddenly, as Don snored soundly in the bunk below him, there really was something he could do about it. The thought kept him awake awhile considering, but finally he slept.

The following day he was on duty in the library as usual and, in between dishing out books ranging from *Ptolemy's Guide to Teleportation* and *Journey to the centre of the Earth* to Mills and Boon romances, he had time for a chat with one of the wardens. He had been lucky with Fred Cornish, he was a mild-mannered man who, uniform apart, had the appearance of an absent minded academic and, unlike many of his colleagues, had always seemed concerned for the welfare of the prisoners in his charge. He had helped Bernie get some training on the computer, saying it might help him when he got out. He had also got him his comfortable job in the library; he'd never believed Bernie when he had claimed to be innocent, they never spoke of it though the warden knew all the circumstances of Bernie's conviction. Certainly, he had always treated the escape plan as a joke, regularly asking that he be sent a postcard "once you are outside".

And, of course, innocent Bernie was not. He had taken part in the robbery even though it was not his idea and he had been egged on by the wrong mates. His part was a minor one, but the job had gone wrong, they had been discovered at the warehouse and one of the team had hit the discoverer. His sentence had increased because of someone else's ill-judged violent action. All these lies. Sometimes he wondered why he said these things: that he was innocent, that he would escape, and that he had made no money from the job when in fact one of the team had got away and money was waiting for him on the outside, also that he had... no hang on, he thought, he had to get real. But he found he did now have an idea and reckoned that something just might be possible, even if there was more to be done. He resolved to say nothing about his plans to Don, they had become good friends and if he wanted to surprise anyone, then he wanted to surprise Don. He continued to mull over his idea, but he would need some help to make it possible. An hour or so into the shift Fred Cornish was doing his rounds.

"Morning, Breakout – bit late this morning, weren't you? That's not like you."

"Morning, Mr Cornish, sorry, I know I was a couple of minutes behind, but it's my anniversary today and I got a bit of ribbing about it at breakfast – you know, about my escape plan and all."

"I dare say, but you and I know it's just a joke don't we, behave yourself and you'll be out of here soon enough, you're doing okay, I wouldn't have got you on that computer course otherwise."

"Yeah, and thanks for that, Mr Cornish. You're one of the good ones and I'm grateful. You've always looked out for me. I appreciate it; when I do get out – properly that is – I don't want ever to come back inside. I am only in here in the first place because I got in with the wrong company. If that psycho Stan hadn't hit that guy, I would have been out already. He's a right nutter."

"Well, yes, he sounds like a bad one for sure, but he's not here in this prison so you've no need to see him again. Come on now, Breakout, you've work to do"

A year later, Bernie was still incarcerated when the anniversary joshing came round again at breakfast.

"One more year, Breakout. How's the plan coming?"

"Still here, are you? We'll have to change your name to 'Stayput'."

It was good humoured banter but this time he didn't just smile, he responded, shouting over his shoulder to one wit.

"All right, All right, but I might really have an idea this time. Just wait... You'd miss me if I did get out wouldn't you, eh, Don?" He turned to focus on Don who was sitting alongside him as usual.

"Nah, be glad to see the back of you! No. Yup, I suppose I would, so just don't you go without telling me, eh." He chuckled.

"But I *keep on* telling you. You'll see: one day you'll find I'm just gone, so don't be surprised when I am and don't say I didn't warn you."

"You reckon? Come on, finish your breakfast or we'll be late for our work sessions – off to the library again are you, lucky devil?" That comment Bernie did defend.

"The library may seem like a cushy number, but it's work too you know, besides it's fascinating to see what people borrow. Half of the books I sign out are crime novels, I sometimes think people hope to pick up tips that will prevent them being caught next time. And did I tell you that old 'Tattoo' Thomson is a Mills and Boon fan, you wouldn't credit it, would you?"

Later in the library Bernie stamped a book and muttered, "there you go then," as his fellow prisoner departed. He looked up as the warden approached the desk.

"Excuse me, Mr Cornish, can you spare me a moment?"

"Yes, Breakout, what can I do for you?"

"Can I ask you what you think? I've been doing All right here in the library, haven't I?"

"Well, yes, no problem. You're keeping up with the computer course I signed you up for too, aren't you? If I wasn't such a hard taskmaster, I would say that you're pretty much the ideal prisoner!" Fred Cornish seemed to be in mellow mood.

"If I've kept my nose clean and behaved well it's largely down to you Mr Cornish, you've always been on my side so far as you can, right?"

"I do try and help those who I feel can be helped, you know – those that deserve it. That computer business will stand you in good stead when you get out."

"Yes, I know you've helped many of us and I, for one, do really appreciate it. Do you mind if I ask you something? It's, well it's just an idea but…"

A few nights later Bernie had things to do. Luckily his cell mate slept like the dead. Bernie had found his snoring annoying over the years, only their friendship and a pair of industrial strength earplugs, suggested and brought in by his wife, had stopped them falling out. Now, as he moved silently about the cell, he was happy that the chances of Don waking up were virtually nil. Soon he was ready, only a few minutes to go and then, the signal came at precisely 5.00 a.m. – and he slipped quietly out of the cell, a satchel-style bag hung over his shoulder. Don snored on unaware.

A while later Don woke slowly, he rubbed a stubbly chin and called out his usual "Morning Breakout", but then quickly became aware that he was alone in the cell. Of his cellmate there was no sign. He looked round the small space again unbelievingly, but Bernie was gone. Don was flabbergasted, it wasn't possible – where was he? He muttered under his breath:

"Well, I'll be... can you really have escaped, Breakout?"

A little later when the cells were opened for the day it was Fred Cornish who turned the key.

"Where's your friend?" He said at once, seeing Don alone in the cell. Don just shrugged; he was still in shock and could think of absolutely nothing to say. A moment later the door was slammed shut again and, leaving Don inside, the warden hurried away down the corridor and disappeared.

It was a strange day and normal routine was largely abandoned. Don spent most of it locked up and still not knowing what to think and all he could get Fred to say, when he saw him in the afternoon, was, "We don't know where he is."

Gradually, as the rumour mill went to work, it became clear that Bernie was no longer in the prison; he had, well, it appeared the only conclusion possible was that he had broken out. Three days later Don received a postcard from him. The message consisted of only two words above a scrawled signature: "Told you." He had written, with the words followed by three exclamation marks. By the end of the day every single prison inmate regarded Bernie as a legend.

In a small town fifty or so miles from the prison Bernie's

wife Mary poured him another cup of tea and sliced him a large portion of home-made cake.

"It's so good to have you back, love." She had repeated this mantra umpteen times over the last few days, this time adding, "but no more capers, eh, I don't want to lose you again."

"Yeah, okay, I promise." Bernie meant it too; he had no intention of returning to prison.

"You are a card though, Bernie," Mary continued. "Your whole time inside seems to have been based on lies: saying you were innocent and that you would escape, well really, but I guess it made a tough time a little easier. You were lucky with Don, an ideal cellmate it seems, and that Fred Cornish was always good to you, wasn't he?"

"Yeah, Don is a good mate, and Fred Cornish really helped, especially as I came out, well, without him I couldn't... anyway he entered into my little plan right proper he did. He thought it was a great joke. Mind you, what really made it possible was that I'd told everyone that I was to serve a *seven* year sentence when it was in fact only *six,* less time off for good behaviour. Everyone thought my release date was further ahead and when the actual date came Fred Cornish slipped me out of my cell in the early morning. I left Don asleep and snoring. We crept along the corridors, and I was at Reception all set to go before anyone else was awake. No one saw me. Now I can't wait to see Don's face when I visit! Fred Cornish's promised he won't say anything to anyone, in fact everyone will think I escaped until I go to visit Don."

"Visiting time is a week away you know. Poor Don, what *is* he going to say when he sees you?" Mary tried to imagine the scene.

"I've sent him a postcard; he'll get that before I go to visit. It had a picture of Dover Castle on it – you know, where the cross-channel ferries go to France from."

"Yes, you told me. Poor Don, that's almost cruel – now can I get you some more tea and another slice of cake, love?"

"Yes, thanks, that would be very nice. And Mary... do you think you could bake a cake for me to take for Don when I visit; maybe then he won't actually kill me!"

I wrote "Disappearing trick" as a short story and it was later rewritten as a short play to be entered in a competition at my local radio station BBC Radio Essex. The play was not placed in the top three, though I did hear later from the presenter that it was one that they felt had merit. More important, it later proved the inspiration for my fourth novel, "Once a thief", in which a slightly modified Bernie became a significant character. As ever, where ideas for fiction come from remains something of a mystery to most writers.

Brushing away the past

He moved forward slowly and steadily, his eyes scanning from side to side as he planted his feet with care amidst the rubble, which shifted disconcertingly as he moved. The crash had occurred only hours ago, a small plane had overshot the runway and had come down doing substantial damage to the nearby village. All around buildings were in different states of collapse: some virtually untouched, others worse than the building he now moved across. He climbed over a long concrete beam and saw that the specially trained dog that preceded him had stopped and was nosing into a crevice. Its tail raised high and wagging, it seemed to have found something – or rather someone – and given it's training that meant someone was still alive.

Harry caught up with the dog, moved his feet into what seemed stable positions and crouched down. He looked around him and called out. "Quiet everyone." Then he shouted into the crevice. "Is anyone there? Can you hear me?"

He had attended many disasters and such moments could be heart-stopping when a sound was heard amongst the devastation, one indicating the chance of a survivor having been found and the possibility that a life might be saved. He stooped lower and listened. Presently he heard a faint reply.

"Hello. Help me – please help me." The voice was clearly female, and she sounded young.

"Help's coming, how are you?" He called back.

"I'm okay, but it's dark. I can't move."

"Is anyone else there?" He continued his fact finding. The voice sounded faint, distant, but though weak it was clear and audible.

"Only Billy."

"Is Billy All right?" There was silence for a moment... then: "He says he is, but he's got cobwebs on his face, and he hates spiders."

Harry added reassurance, insisting it was probably just dust, he repeated that help was near, he asked her name and was told it was Jenny.

"We'll have you out of there soon," he said. "Just let me tell people where you are."

He stood up carefully. Around him scores of people, clad in fluorescent jackets like his and wearing yellow hard hats moved across the buildings near him, rescue vehicles threaded their way amongst the rubble and sirens wailed in the background. On several wrecked houses flames were being doused and smoke rose through the dusty air. Only the tail fin of the plane was recognisable, the short fuselage was buried in a row of cottages. Harry called out and began to get things organised. Although Jenny was apparently not too deeply buried, lifting equipment would be necessary, and within minutes other men had gathered around and a crane was positioned carefully.

"Hello Jenny, we're digging now," he called down into the rubble. "Are you still All right?"

The voice was still faint. "Yes, I think so, and Billy says we'll be okay."

"How're you doing, Billy?" he called.

Again, there was a long pause before Jenny replied, "He says we're fine."

"Can he shout to me?" Another pause. "No, he doesn't want to talk."

Harry wondered if that meant Billy was in some way injured but decided not to mention that possibility.

"Okay, not long now." The rubble around was gently being moved, with care so as not to precipitate any further collapse. A large concrete beam was unearthed, and the crane was able to lift that clear making further digging by hand much easier.

"Nearly there," he called. There was no reply. He called again, moments later the voice answered, but it was weaker now.

"Please hurry, Billy hates the cobwebs."

Caught up in all that it was necessary to do Harry had only thought of the person as a live one to be saved, now listening to the weak little voice he was more convinced that Jenny sounded young. "How old are you?" He called. Again, a pause "I'm five and a half, but Billy's older, he's looking after me."

"That's good – how old's Billy then?"

He tried to keep the conversation going and wanted to ask about parents and perhaps begin taking steps to reunite the family. If Jenny's parents were alive somewhere they would be distraught, wondering where the kids were and if they had survived.

But there was no reply.

He called and called but neither Jenny nor Billy answered. Nothing further was heard as the careful digging continued, and a little over an hour later they reached the body of the little girl. She laid curled up face down, protected under a heavy wooden table, but her leg had received a gash and, without knowing it, she had bled to death, her face was coated in the dust she had feared was cobwebs. She was one of dozens of people killed in the accident, but to Harry she was special. He knew he would remember her quavering voice until his dying day.

But what about Billy? Jenny was alone, but when

they gently lifted out her little body, there, clutched in her arms, was a teddy bear, rather old by the look of it and with one eye conspicuously askew. The bear was grimy with dust, but Harry could see it wore a sky-blue t-shirt with the word "Billy" on it. Later Harry would pass it on to those collecting the various personal effects unearthed as the rescue crew worked on; meantime a shout and a barking dog pulled his attention elsewhere.

A year later and many thousands of miles distant Mary drove a battered open-topped Land Rover across the African bush. Dressed in khaki, her wheels threw up red dust, which rose in her wake as she headed for the orphanage located in a small village twenty miles from her current base. A young Oxfam volunteer, she was part of a team installing fresh water supplies around villages in the area, but this was her little private project. She collected things for the orphanage and made a monthly trip to visit them bringing whatever little extras she could to help the children – all of whom had been rescued from difficult pasts, but who were now safe and whose lives were now getting closer to normality.

The hot sun burnt down from high in the cloudless sky, and she arrived at the cluster of tin roofed buildings in late morning, ready for a break and a refreshing drink. She parked outside the main residence and in the shade of a tree but was only half out of the vehicle before she was surrounded by a crowd of bright-eyed children laughing and cheering.

"Give me a minute," she said grinning at them as she fixed her unruly hair into a ponytail and put on a sun hat. The children knew Mary's visits meant presents and their excitement was palpable. Deciding to put her drink on hold, Mary called out cheery hellos, moved to the back of the Land Rover and began to unload battered, much-used cardboard boxes. These held everything from clothes to kitchen utensils and brightly coloured mugs. But one box was special, it held toys she had collected from various well-wishers.

"You can all have something from here," she said. "Just one thing each mind. Make sure everyone gets something."

Smiling and laughing the children fell on the box like starving jackals and each of them ran off with something: simple things: a spinning top, a kite, a jigsaw puzzle and more. Little Nelson, clad in bleached denim shorts and a faded red t-shirt was last to approach the box. He had been found abandoned and badly beaten before being taken in by the orphanage and still walked with a pronounced limp, one bare foot dragging a little behind the other; though he was improving every day, he could not yet cope with the scrum around the box. But one toy was left.

"What have you found?" Mary asked, worried that his being last might have short-changed him.

"A teddy bear Miss," he said, adding, "Thank you." The bear looked a bit battered and sported a t-shirt showing that its name was Billy.

"He's called Billy," said Mary pointing out the letters to Nelson, who at six was now just starting to read.

Nelson studied the bear intently in the way only a six-year-old can do, he turned it slowly from side to side and then clutched it firmly to his chest. Immediately he pulled it away from himself and yelled. "Cobwebs, cobwebs! I hate spiders!"

Mary lent forward and brushed the bear's face. "Don't worry. It's just dust," she said. "No spiders, he *is* rather old, I'm afraid. I'll help you clean him up later."

Nelson turned the bear so they were face to face just a few inches apart.

"He's fine," he said. "But... he does have a rather a

sad face. I'll cheer him up and I'm sure we will soon be special friends. We'll look after each other forever."

Neither Mary nor Nelson knew anything of Billy's history, of course, but after his trauma of a year ago and having spent the subsequent months in darkness – shut away in boxes that had ultimately crossed the world – he looked as if he might agree wholeheartedly with Nelson's comments. Indeed, maybe he would say so later... when he and Nelson had got to know each other a little better.

Maybe I should apologise for this being a sad one. "Brushing away the past" is another story that had competition success. I seem to remember that the theme of the competition was "Cobwebs"; perhaps an indication that such a theme does not need to be central to a story, though it should be clearly respected. This story appears in the book mentioned in the introduction which was produced as a fundraiser for Farleigh Hospice, "A Great Little Gallimaufry".

A night to remember

"Right, Ladies and Gentlemen, my name is Peter Spillman, and I would like to welcome you here on this special night."

The here in question was the chapel-like dining hall of Banham Manor, a minor stately home of no great import other than having a reputation for being haunted. It was the night of Hallow'en and I had come with a friend to the party organised by the Hall's owners, one at which, come midnight, those attending were promised the possibility of a ghostly experience.

"I'm not really sure about this you know," I said to my friend John, who sat alongside me and had been the instigator of my attending the event. This was billed as "A Bump in the Night Night at Banham Hall." John held up a finger and shushed me as our host, a young man of about thirty, wearing a tweed jacket, who was the son of the elderly owner, again addressed the 50 or 60 people in the room.

"There is food and drink first," he said, "but eat up because just ahead of midnight we will dim the lights and it is then that there is often an appearance." He drew out the word: app-ear-ance in a way that put an exaggerated emphasis on it.

"I can't promise anything," he said – and indeed the small print in Banham Manor's literature made that clear – and he continued: "But this time last year we had the full works, noises, a chill in the air and an actual apparition which crossed the hall just over there." He gave a slow exaggerated point across the space in front of him and every eye in the room obediently looked in that direction.

As he finished up with, "Enjoy yourselves and eat up," the room filled with chatter and John turned and headed for the buffet, throwing a 'come on then' signal over his shoulder. I followed him towards the long, decorated table, still frankly apprehensive, and by the time I had checked out the beer, a local brew I was pleased to see, and was positioned at the buffet I had lost sight of John completely. As I turned, I bumped into someone, a 'Sorry' springing automatically to my lips. In front of me I found a vision of loveliness holding a glass of white wine and a plate of food. She smiled and I suddenly thought the occasion might not be so bad after all.

With only a split second to think I offered, "You know it's going to be much easier to eat and drink sitting down, shall I see if I can find us a seat?" And you know what? I got a "Yes." And another smile. She had such a wonderful smile. A few moments later we were sitting opposite each other at a table in a corner of the room, still with no sign of John, but despite my apprehension about the event, I was not finding that a downside now.

"Well," I said, "I'm Frank." "I'm Sally," she offered in return and she smiled again. I was sure there was a connection here. She was attractive, blonde hair, a pretty face and a long flowing dress that hinted at a great figure, but there was something about her beyond that – I was sure she was nice, I was sure we would get on, well, almost sure, but I wondered what to say next. Then: "I'm not really sure about this ..." We uttered the same phrase in unison, and both of us laughed out loud.

"So why did you come?" I asked. Her situation was, in some ways, similar to mine: John had persuaded me to come to what was my first such event and Sally had been invited by her friend Jane. Said friend was as little in evidence as John; we even wondered as we chattered on if they were sitting together somewhere else in the room. It was difficult to see clearly. Peter had dimmed the lights a little once most people had settled to eating and drinking. Anyway, I did not really care, Sally was a find, and I hoped that our meeting, albeit in rather odd circumstances, would be more than a momentary one. I had not actually said, "Do you have a boyfriend?" but there was no sign of any such from our chat, and we appeared to be getting on fine.

Then, it seemed like in no time at all, it was approaching midnight. Peter announced that the lights would now be dimmed further and asked that everyone keep silent. A moment later somewhere in the house a clock struck twelve. The whole room sat quietly, as the chimes were the only sound and, as I looked around, I spotted John through the gloom sitting a little way off across the room; he was with a chap I knew he had once worked with, perhaps someone else he had persuaded to attend. He pointed at Sally, nodded vigorously and was clearly indicating approval. Just then there was a noise above our heads and the boards creaked. Then the lights flickered a bit and I whispered to Sally, "I'm sure we don't need to be worried." She said nothing, though she looked a little apprehensive and just smiled back, but she also gave my hand a brief squeeze. As I dwelt on the possible significance of her touch the air around us seemed to chill suddenly, it was sufficient to bring a number of gasps and some mutterings from around the room. Next moment the room was in turmoil, the lights began a constant flickering, three large chandeliers hanging low from the high ceiling began to swing and creaked as they did so, and the vigorous banging from the floor above returned with a vengeance. A significant number of people gasped or shouted, one woman screamed, and many got to their feet, milling about as the lights then went out completely and the room was suddenly almost completely dark, only a slight glow from a skylight high in the roof gave evidence of a moon outside.

Peter yelled for people to keep calm, but it made only a trivial difference to the level of noise and I'm afraid I just freaked out. This was not what I had expected. I couldn't bear for Sally to see me in a state, so I leapt up and bolted from the room. I just needed a moment to calm myself, I hoped Sally would barely notice my absence in the furore and the darkness, and John was too far away to see I had lost it. In the long passageway connecting the Hall to the outside world I stood unmoving trying to calm myself. Then I started as there was a sudden voice at my elbow: John, just visible in the dim light as it was a little less dark here than in the main Hall. He must have followed me out.

"You okay?" he said, "You look like you've seen a ghost." He gave a cheeky laugh, perhaps trying to lighten the moment. That was no help at all, and certainly not the great joke he clearly thought it was. I did now, I must confess, feel somewhat silly, but then I had never been at an event like this before and, despite John's briefing, I really had no experience of what to expect.

"Come on," said John pointing towards the Hall, "we need to get back in there. I love these evenings, anything to break the monotony, right? I saw you with a rather nice young lady, didn't I? Had a good chat, did you? It's always good to meet new people." I realised that I had nearly forgotten about Sally; John was right, I had to get back inside. Off we set through the gloom, I tried to remember exactly where I had been sitting and did so very accurately too, wondering if Sally would have realised I had been gone. It had only been a couple of minutes after all, but when I located my seat, I did not get that lovely smile again, the flickering light showed that she was staring at me wide-eyed and with a horrified expression on her face and I wondered what had gone on in my absence. Then I realised her look was directed at me: without thinking I had followed John as he led the way back into the Hall, and he had brought us floating straight through the wall. Another potential beautiful friendship stillborn.

The theme here needs no explanation and is one that is a staple of the short story genre, indeed it also regularly features as a competition theme, and that may be how I came to write this one.

Who'd be a writer?

"I'm not very happy…" The figure that was clearly a ghost spoke in a deep, dry, rasping voice, seemingly that of someone who had not spoken for an awfully long time.

The second-hand bookshop was quaint, the building old and promising of a labyrinthine layout inside. Set at the far end of the short high street, it looked to be closed as I approached, seeking shelter as the weather deteriorated, the dark ominous sky and scudding clouds unleashing rain whipped sideways by a sudden wind that increased in vehemence by the moment, sending the trees on the empty plot alongside the shop into a frenzy of whirling branches. It was late on a winter afternoon and the shop window was not lit so, with no real confidence that it would still be open, I tried the door, hoping to spend a little time browsing and that the storm would abate soon.

The door was not locked, and I hurried inside, bringing a few wet leaves with me.

Beyond a dark lobby that from outside had contributed to my thinking that the place was closed, the shop opened up and was lit just enough to make the layout visible. I shook water from my coat and stepped forward. I could see no sign of anyone and called out: "Hello, anyone there? Are you open?" There was no answer, and I repeated the call. Again, I received only silence.

I could see a table spread with books in front of me

and, as moments passed, I found I could read the titles as my eyes became accustomed to the low light and I could see also the ranks of shelves beyond. To my right was a table with a cash register at its centre, behind it a chair on which a cardigan hung; no one was on duty there and I was still unsure whether the shop was open or closed. To my left an open staircase rose to allow access to a mezzanine floor: a balcony that ran round half the room backed by floor-to-ceiling shelves packed with books. High above the light was even dimmer, though I could read the sign at the foot of the stairs that offered the invitation: "Much more Fiction."

Approaching the till table, I called out again, but the silence continued. I saw a lamp on the desk, lent down and clicked it on. The light in the shop increased a little, though it mainly pooled on the desk, and I could see no more switches that would allow me to increase it further. I returned to the shop entrance, looked out and found the rain as bad as ever. As I stood there the street beyond lit up for a moment; lightning had been added to the mix and was quickly followed by the throaty rumble of thunder. There might be no one about, but I concluded that with the door unlocked I could browse for a while as planned until the owner returned; I imagined they were probably somewhere in the back making a cuppa. They no doubt anticipated few customers given that the weather outside had left the street deserted.

As I turned again towards the shelves, I thought I heard a sound up on the mezzanine floor, but looking up and along the gloomy balcony I could see nothing, and the sound did not repeat.

The heavy cloud exaggerated the low light in the shop; lightning flashed again briefly and lit up the room a little. I saw dark wooden panelling lining the staircase, which rose from the main floor in an upward curve, upstairs shadows rippled into the far corners.

The thunder that followed the lightning died away leaving the place eerily silent, yet not completely devoid of noise. The wood of stairs and floors in what was clearly an old building gave out occasional random creaks, no doubt due to temperature changes, and currently as the weather deteriorated it was getting colder. There were moments when some sounds could have been taken for footsteps as the boards above shifted a little and again I glanced at the mezzanine.

I love books, I love to browse, indeed I rarely emerge from a bookshop without buying something. Besides I'm a writer, and always look for my own books in any shop I visit. But alone in this quiet shop, I began to wonder if I should have come in. Increasingly the place seemed a little odd, the low light, the silence and the lack of anyone staffing the shop all contributed to it feeling somewhat weird. I tried to concentrate on the titles in front of me on the entrance table, then definite sounds from above startled me. This time there was no doubt: there was somebody moving about. I called out again: "Hello, is the shop open?" But the words died in my throat as I turned to face the continuing sound.

The figure I could now see on the stairs was tall, his dress was old fashioned, a long dark jacket hung loosely on his lean frame and his trousers seemed to sort of peter out into mistiness near the floor. His hair was long, and a curiously neat beard covered his face. He appeared as if being only in his thirties and looked resigned, bored even, as if engaged in an endless and tedious mission.

But it was an overall lack of clarity that made it obvious he must be a ghost. He appeared to kind of fray at the edges, becoming misty, without any clear definition of where he ended. Besides, he had no feet. Against whatever background he moved there were patches where he was almost, but not quite, transparent. Another flicker of lightning showed this aspect of his being more clearly for a moment and the thunder that followed seemed to echo round the whole shop. His credentials as a ghost were not in doubt and he appeared ominous and threatening too in a way that more than overcame my scepticism. Why was he here? What was he going to do?

Still standing in front of the table I watched as the figure began to come slowly down the stairs then paused motionless a few steps from the bottom. He seemed uncertain what to do next. His head turned to focus on me, the misty yet piercing blue eyes aimed towards me alone. Then the figure spoke.

"I'm not very happy... not very happy with the... the picture you paint of me."

"Who... m... me?" I found I was stuttering.

"Well, you're writing about my appearance, aren't you?"

"I guess so, but ...."

"Yes, you are, who else, I'm just a figment of your imagination." True enough I suppose.

"Well, you're a ghost, so figment is probably an appropriate word."

"I have to say, it's not very satisfactory. I'm just fixed here on the page, all I do is what you decide I should do, it's not very fulfilling... it's not in the least exciting. Indeed, all I ever seem to have done is walk slowly around this old shop. Frankly it's boring and, what's more, you imply I've been doing it for a great many years. There must be something more interesting I can do. You've made me look properly ghostly after all, though I have to say that this place is a huge cliché and as to the weather, well it's hardly original, is it? But let's get back to my appearance, shall we? Look at me, I don't mind the inherent ghostliness, that's par for the course I think, and it could be worse, I might be disfigured or goblin-like, but I just sort of fade away at the bottom, you've not bothered to write me any legs, only a misty indistinctness near the ground. It makes walking about somewhat difficult. When I try to take a step forward, it just doesn't feel right. You've got proper legs. Who wrote those? Maybe they can help."

"No one wrote my legs, they came, well, they came with the rest of me... besides a misty connection with the ground is traditional for ghosts. I'm just following convention. Wait a minute. Why are we having this conversation? You shouldn't be able to speak without my writing your words."

"Are you writing them?"

"Yes. No... I'm not sure..." This was, it occurred to me, becoming seriously bizarre. Very weird hardly described it. Another flash of lightning lit up the room, quickly followed by thunder again rolling round the sky, for a moment drowning out the sound of the drumming rain. The figure's face became clearer, almost as if he was drawing strength from the storm.

"Ah, then maybe I do have some free will after all, maybe my vague substance and lack of proper legs isn't holding me back. Maybe I can really do something for myself now. Something more interesting and frankly more fitting for a ghost too. Write me some action, let me get down to some serious haunting. Let me envelop someone and reduce them to dust. Go on, set up a situation but let me decide how it develops." The dry voice was getting stronger.

"I'm certainly not going to make you lethal. Actually, I'm really not sure what to write next. I think I've got writers' block. I just can't think what I should make you do."

"You could just leave it to me."

"What do you mean, leave it to you?"

"Let me decide everything. I can think of things to do, I can think of a great many things to do. And do you know what, I do believe this writers' block of yours is giving me strength. Even walking is easier now. Look." The figure moved down the remaining stairs.

"But I didn't write that you walked."

"No, you didn't, did you, nor that I speak to you, this seems to be a real step forward for me. Now what shall I do next? I've got so many ideas."

"I'm the one who has the ideas."

"But not anymore it seems. I'm definitely getting stronger. I can move at will now. See."

The figure took a couple more steps towards me; its legs seemingly more distinct now, and its appearance much more threatening. Again, lightning lit the scene and seemed to add substance to the apparition. The figure paused until the thunder that followed had died away, then continued moving towards me. I stepped back sharply knocking a number of books off the table to form an untidy heap on the floor.

"Yes, it seems to me that there's so much I am able to do now. And do on my own. First, I shall get out of this place, or rather off this page. I know I can do it, regardless of what you write. I might wait for a change in the weather though. The fact is I don't think I'll have need of you anymore." The figure moved towards me again and its strengthening voice took on a more menacing tone as it went on: "No need for you whatsoever."

A slightly longer story in the same genre as the last one, this, as a lover of books, I just had to set in a dusty old bookshop. It seems only fair that sometimes the writer can be the protagonist too!

The curious case of the lost umbrella

The Reverend St. John-Beresford rushed from the vicarage to the church clutching a copy of the *Church Times* above his head to give him a little protection from the falling rain. It had been a wet week.

"Biblical rain," he said under his breath thinking it the best description as he wondered for the umpteenth time what had become of his umbrella. He was usually very careful with it; it was a good one and had been a present from a grateful member of his congregation. Now, there was no sign of it, it had just vanished. And he found himself not only wet but also disgruntled as a result. He stamped his feet, conscious that one shoe had been letting in a little water, and removed his coat and shook it before going inside the church.

He was surely too young still to be getting major lapses in memory. He usually remembered why he had gone upstairs, had no great problem with names, though a declining congregation maybe helped with that; the only exception was maybe computer passwords. This he solved by always using the same one, "iRemembered!", for everything. All normal enough, so he was pretty sure he remembered when he had last used his umbrella. He had been driving along the bypass and had seen a police car parked on the edge of the road ahead. They had stopped Gwen Cameron, a stalwart of the church volunteers, he had recognised her aged green Morris

Minor at the roadside. Always disposed to help members of his flock he had pulled up behind them and, because it was raining, pulled out his umbrella, opened it up and gone forward to the policeman. His dog collar introduced him, so all he said, getting down on his knees as he did so and clasping his hand together around the umbrella handle as if in prayer was, "Please be merciful, officer, she's a good woman." He had then returned to his car neither adding another word nor waiting for any reaction from the policeman, he was sure he had stowed away his umbrella on the back seat and had no further recollection of seeing it after that. He had checked in his car twice. It wasn't there.

Inside the church he hung up his coat, left the now soggy newspaper just inside the door and, as he moved down the aisle, he met Gwen again. She was arranging flowers: she ran a rota and the church always looked beautiful even if the roof was poised to leak and a perpetual fund-raising campaign was necessary to keep ahead of its steady deterioration.

"Oh, hello Vicar," she said at once, "thank you so much for speaking to that policeman, whatever were you thinking? You must have got your knees all wet. Anyway, the policeman couldn't stop laughing. He let me off with a warning. I was only going 35 after all." She chuckled.

"I'm glad it helped. Now something else Gwen: You know my umbrella is missing," he said, speaking to Gwen as she continued to arrange her flowers. "I've looked everywhere, and I can only conclude that someone must have stolen it. I thought it was in my car, but it's not and when I visit the church, I usually leave it propped up in the porch just outside the main door, so, it spends some time there unattended and it being taken from there is, I think, now regrettably the only explanation."

"I suppose it's possible," said Gwen, skilfully

inserting bright red blooms into the vase in front of her. "But sadly I suppose that makes it likely that whoever stole it is one of your parishioners."

"Oh dear, yes, you could be right," said the reverend, shaking his head and wondering what he could do about that; he didn't like to think there was a thief in their midst.

But Gwen continued and she had a thought: "I know what you should do," she said, her voice adopting a tone projecting unchallengeable logic. "You should use a sermon to prompt its return, something about theft; it will make any perpetrator feel so guilty that either their guilt will be evident, or they will unobtrusively return your umbrella to its accustomed place."

The Reverend St. John-Beresford muttered a polite response and went about his business, but later he found himself thinking that Gwen might have a point. Later that day he took the verger into his confidence and asked him about her idea. He considered it for a moment, taking his time, he was of an age when everything had to be taken at a steady pace.

"Might work," he said finally. "If you give people something really strident from the pulpit, say a review of the Ten Commandments with suitable stress on 'thou shalt not steal', then that might just do the trick. Yes, Gwen may well be right. It's worth a try, I think. And, who knows, it might just get your umbrella back." He looked well content with his pronouncement.

The Reverend St. John-Beresford was in fine form the following Sunday. The umbrella had not reappeared, and his sermon had been carefully prepared: his notes outlined a review of the Ten Commandments with particular emphasis on that denouncing stealing. A commanding figure in the pulpit his words echoed round the church and the power of his oratory was strong. This was the same reverend who had brought a significant proportion of his congregation to tears at the recent funeral service for Archibald Brown, a long term and much-loved resident of the parish, and at a recent christening too. He could certainly turn on the emotion when required. There were moments when his voice made Charlton Heston seem like a shrinking violet. But he knew not to go on for too long, his parishioners' patience was not infinite, and he knew also that his predecessor in the post had had a reputation for sermons that made eternity seem like a split-second. Because of this, his greater brevity always commanded attention. Today the members of the congregation hung on every word as the commandment countdown went down from ten to one.

As they stood at the church door after the service the verger complimented him on "another stirring sermon" but he also expressed considerable puzzlement.

"You went through all the commandments," he said slowly, "but you dismissed stealing in a single sentence. That was the one you were going to emphasise. Whatever happened? This was supposed to get your umbrella returned, remember?" Before the Reverend St. John-Beresford could reply to him a crack of thunder rent the air as the church windows lit up with flickering lightning; the rain was starting again and the storm appeared to be right overhead. Looking a bit sheepish, the reverend could not take this as a very good sign.

"Well, yes, you're right," he said when the noise outside had subsided, "that is what I planned to do." He paused, then continued in a more conspiratorial tone. "But you know what, during the sermon, when I got to adultery I suddenly remembered where I'd left my umbrella."

I hope no one is offended by the thought of an adulterous vicar, but I could not resist including this one. I take no credit for the story. It is an old joke and what I have written here is the result of a writing group brief to turn a joke into a short story. Incidentally, many years ago my mother really did approach a policeman in this way and the friend stopped for speeding was let off with a warning. Mind you, she was a trifle eccentric, and it was many years ago. I do not recommend the same methodology these days!

Bus stop

It's just as well I hate dogs, well, a certain kind of dog anyway, otherwise, well I... but I'm getting ahead of myself. I recently started a new job and moved into a new flat. I'm now working in London and that's great, but wow it's expensive. I finally found a small flat that I could afford (just) and it's very nice, but the compromise is that I have a bit of a bus journey to get to the office.

I go through it all in zombie mode, kind of switching off for the duration of the journey and spending most of the time buried in a book. There's not too much problem getting on the bus where I board; I always get a seat. I'm getting used to it but a few things I do notice. For instance, I now recognise several people who travel regularly at a similar time to me. The man with an aversion to washing, whose BO I avoid, the middle-aged woman with the amazing hairdo, something I imagine must be a failed experiment, though so far she's sticking with it, the woman with the pushchair the size of a small tank and the younger woman with the dog.

The latter is a bit more of a puzzle. First the dog is simply horrid. What kind of woman would carry a dog in a carpet bag? What kind of woman would choose to own a pug-faced rat-like creature of this sort anyway? It has a bow on its head for goodness sake – gross, inappropriate and just, well, plain yuck. Initially, the first time I saw it, I let myself imagine – hope if I'm honest – that she was taking it to some sort of disposal centre. I supposed it deserves respect as a living creature so perhaps I should add the hope that disposal would be humane and cause it no great suffering. But I suppose, however difficult I found it to believe, and it really was a thoroughly unpleasant creature, she might actually take some sort of perverse pleasure in owning it. Each to their own.

Anyway, it was not my favourite creature, not by a very long way. So far, though I see the woman regularly, it has always been at a distance.

Today as I sat on the bus on the way to work, I looked up from my book and found that dog-lady was taking the seat next to me. Up close the creature was even more horrid. I didn't know where she went of a morning, surely, she wasn't taking the wretched thing to work, I thought. Perhaps the bag was to protect the other occupants of the bus, though its head was sticking out and a rank and unpleasant smell was drifting around, becoming stronger in the confined space and overpowering for me in the next seat. The woman was in any case ignoring the dog and was busy with her phone; ninety percent of the passengers were doing something on their phone, watching something, listening to something – something raucous in the case of the youth sitting immediately in front of me who had the volume sufficiently high to cause both a leakage of sound from his headphones and him deafness in later years. A few people were even actually making phone calls; most of those speaking at the top of their voice. Dog-lady's fingers flew to and fro on the screen as her dog's smell continued to waft around her, and around me. I had reckoned she might be foreign, she was probably in her early thirties, though wrapped up against the cold as she was it was difficult to judge much about her. But the people around me made an eclectic group; a sign of the times I guess in an increasingly cosmopolitan capital the population of which included people from all over the world. I returned to my book and to following the unwritten rule of travel in the capital that people ignore each other, a rule adhered to pretty much universally in the early morning when many people are still half asleep. The dog's smell got worse. Why did she have to come on this particular bus? Why did she have to sit next to me?

Then I heard the dog snuffle alongside me, followed by a sudden sneeze. I looked up and saw a cloud of spray bursting forth from its nose and mouth and drifting widely before sinking towards the floor. Why did the wretched dog have a cold, I thought, as I raised my book higher in front of my face? Then, as I glanced round, I saw the woman had apparently ignored it – and its effect on others, she appeared to have finished with her phone and was sitting gazing out of the window, I presumed to see what point in her journey she had reached while her concentration had been focussed elsewhere. I looked around too wondering if there was a seat I could move to away from the increasingly unpleasant smell. But I had left it too late, the bus was full at this stage. No chance.

Anyway, just then the bus drew to a halt. We were now in the heart of the West End and I realised that my own journey was nearly over. I decided to get off one stop early and walk the last stretch; London air was hardly fresh, but at least I could shake off the awful dog stench before I got to the office.I put my book away in my satchel, got up and disembarked. On the pavement I pushed through a crowd of people waiting to board. The bus was going to be even more crowded now, and I set off down the road resolving to change seats quickly if the woman ever sat near me again; if I did that in the early part of the journey there would be other options, maybe if I went and sat on the upper deck she would never do that and I could then enjoy an odour free journey. The woman's mysterious attraction to the horrid dog remained a mystery to me.

As I walked on, putting the matter out of my mind and thinking of my imminent first moments in the office, unseen back on the bus the woman with the dog put down her phone and reached into her basket. Later my view of that dog changed radically, for despite the distance now existing between myself and the bus, I was still knocked off my feet by the explosion.

"Bus stop" turns out to be dark, though the scenario with the dog was based on a real experience at a time when I lived in London and sometimes got a bus to work.

Radical treatment

My mind raced. A huge alien spacecraft appeared to be on a collision course with me. It was closing fast. I pressed the firing button, seeing green lines of laser fire shoot out towards it but bounce harmlessly off some sort of force field. The craft came on relentlessly, finally it loomed right in front of me, and my view changed silently into a flash of blinding white light.

I woke up, the sheets tangled around my legs and the sun streaming in through the bedroom window. I was dreaming. One of many a night spent mostly tossing and turning and regularly punctuated by bizarre dreams. Months of really bad sleep finally had me going to the doctor. He was, frankly, no great help, being very much against my taking sleeping pills and stressing that it was better to get to the root of the problem. Unsurprisingly an appointment with any kind of counsellor would be many months ahead. Too long, much too long. The problem was affecting my whole life, with my work becoming a real struggle – I had to do something about it. If the GP wouldn't take my problem seriously, then I would have to find another route. Time to go online.

Thus, in due course, with serious sleep deprivation continuing, I found myself checking in at the Rest-right Sleep Clinic, their promise of being able to reset your sleep pattern sounded good to me. Many, now presumably well-rested, clients gave testimonials in praise of their expertise. I signed up and made an appointment for a weekend of observation and assessment. Once checked in I had to fill in a lengthy questionnaire, not only about my sleep problem but about my general health and all sorts of other personal details that I did not see the relevance of to my sleep problem. Then, following a medical check, I quickly discovered that the process proper started with some serious monitoring. I slept there for two nights wired up to various monitors and with surveillance cameras focused on my every toss and turn. And there were plenty of those to monitor; if anything, I found it was even more difficult to sleep in such an odd and unfamiliar environment.

On the morning of the third day, I had an appointment with one of the clinic's doctors. He looked very much the part. A tall distinguished looking man, probably in his early fifties, he wore a white coat and an expression of concern, had a stethoscope round his neck and a name tag proclaiming him to be Dr Gordon. He welcomed me into his consulting room, the plushness of which I realised was being paid for by clients like me.

"Yours is an interesting case," he said, peering at me over huge metal-framed spectacles perched on the end of his nose. Frankly that did not help me one bit, I didn't want him to see me as an extreme sufferer case study. I wanted my case to be a successful one. Treatable. He went on. "We rarely see anyone with such strong and consistent symptoms as you." Just as I thought; hardly news to me.

"So, what next?" I asked. "Is there anything you can do for me?" I thought of the guarantee they had given me. I thought of the substantial fee I had paid. The clinic was clearly not short of a bob or two, the whole place was decorated and furnished to the standard of a first-class hotel, no expense seemed to have been spared in providing comfort for their clients, the food was excellent and the individual bedrooms, despite the profusion of equipment they contained, were very comfortable.

"Certainly, there is. I think we need to give you some radical treatment, I'm afraid it is a somewhat lengthy process, will you be All right to stay on for a few more days?" His gaze directed reassurance at me in spades, his voice had an authority that sounded as if it had been cultivated over many years.

"Is there any extra charge?" This was an immediate worry; I had paid out more than enough already.

"No, no, no." The doctor looked horrified. "We guaranteed that we would make a difference, and don't worry, we stick by that."

"In that case, then it's fine, no one will miss me for a bit." The doctor smiled silently, then looked at me very directly for a long moment.

"We have analysed your details carefully and believe you are ideally suited for this treatment. There is just one thing," he continued. He paused, still smiling. "I must be honest with you. This treatment is new, experimental, in fact, I'm pretty sure the NHS wouldn't approve, well not yet, but we are getting good results, very good results indeed." Again, he turned on the reassurance in a big way; it worked too, he was convincing, and anyway I was beyond desperate.

Such an option needed little thought, I had to do something, the clinic came highly recommended and all my experience there to date had indicated a very professional approach. Dr Gordon's manner reinforced my view. I signed on the dotted line, and we agreed that I would report to the designated treatment room an hour or two later at 3 pm. I just hoped he was right, that this treatment, whatever it was, would make a difference; frankly, given my recent experience, there was not much I would not have tried to get back to sleeping well.

Just after 3pm I was asked to don a robe and lie down in the treatment room, then given a small injection: "just to relax you," I was told by a smiling nurse. That done, I lay back and tried to do just that. Somehow, I felt different, I really was relaxed, I was tired, but then I'm always tired, but I was also becoming distinctly dozy. My eyelids fluttered a couple of times and then comfortably remained closed, I felt that not only did I need to sleep, but that I was going to do just that. My eyelids fluttered open again for a moment, the lights were dimmed, and my vision seemed a little fuzzy, but I could just see two vague white coated figures standing beyond the end of the bed. They seemed to be a man and a woman, but I was not completely sure. As I felt sleep literally unstoppably overpowering me, the last thing I heard was the sound of a brusque female voice.

"Can you hurry this one along, Doctor Gordon, we have an urgent order pending for his lungs."

"Radical Treatment" is another dark one, I know, but I like being able to put a twist in the very last line, something this tale lends itself to doing.

Just a simple signature

"What the..." His voice was a loud spluttering gasp as he woke in a rush. The response had a calming tone.

"Hello, good morning... no, no, don't panic, really, I'm no threat, I'm an angel. I'm here to help."

Martin scrabbled around and found and put on his glasses as sleep rapidly disappeared into the past. His eyes were still blurry with sleep, but the panic in them was totally clear. The figure at the end of his bed remained visible, now clearer, but seemingly surrounded by a slight fuzzy white haze.

Martin sat up, noticing as he did so that the digital time read out by the bed showed 4.05 a.m. He switched on the bedside light. The figure remained visible.

"There is no such thing as... are you real?" He asked. "I'm surely dreaming." He was now sufficiently awake to think what nonsense it was to be speaking out loud; he must, he decided, still be asleep and dreaming. The answer to his question seemed confidently given and even had him doubting his first thought.

"No, you're not dreaming. I am real enough, I'm... well, I'm on a mission and frankly I find myself rather embarrassed."

"Embarrassed? What do you mean?"

"Well, I hate to admit it, but, well, there's been a mistake."

"A mistake?" Martin could still not get his head round what was happening. He shook his head, but the figure remained clearly visible: a tall, slim, classically good-looking man wearing a white suit, white shirt and tie.

"I'm afraid so, it shouldn't happen, especially not in Heaven; things are supposed to run smoothly, in fact I can't remember a single occasion when something similar happened in the past."

"Is that supposed to make me feel better, it's exactly what Ryanair said to me when I had that problem flying to Germany, 'It's never happened before' they said. I didn't care, it didn't make the error any less disruptive to me... Why, why on Earth am I telling you this? Anyway, what mistake are you talking about?"

"Well, as I say it shouldn't have happened, administration is supposed to be efficient, perfectly efficient in fact given where it's taking place, but getting things done can be, I must admit, a little bureaucratic. Frankly the sheer growth of humanity was never envisaged as being so great. Not everyone gets to heaven, of course, and certainly not everyone becomes an angel like me, but even so there are far too many of us. The administration is now so multi-layered – I confess that some of the jobs are... well, frankly some are surplus to requirements. More and more things seem to take an unnecessarily long time, and, in this case, something actually went wrong. Evidently even an angel can make a mistake; who knew. But my job is new and necessary."

"And your job is, what? No wait a minute, I'm finding talking to you from bed more than a touch awkward. Actually, it's weird – can we reconvene in the kitchen? I need coffee. Do you drink coffee?" Martin recognised the absurdity of what he was saying even as he said it.

"I will today, thank you," said the angel. Martin still could not believe what was happening, but he swung his legs out of bed, slipped on his dressing gown and five minutes later they fould themselves sitting on stools at the kitchen worktop sipping coffee.

"Right go on, for goodness sake let's get to the point. Your job is... what exactly?"

"As I said my job is new, I probably shouldn't tell you this, but I have never done this before – you're my first assignment, so please excuse my hesitancy, I have to say that I'm rather feeling my way and it's all a bit embarrassing."

"Can angels be embarrassed?" The figure paused, raised an eyebrow, apparently contemplating the question, and then spoke slowly.

"Well, yes, apparently so. Anyway, let's get on." Martin had led the way downstairs, indicating to the angel that they should sit on a kitchen stool. He had clicked on the kettle and made two cups of coffee, only turning back to deliver the second cup to his mysterious visitor. The figure had still been there, sitting on the stool and was now opening a white folder. Where had that come from Martin wondered, he was sure the figure had not been carrying anything, but now he was somehow opening a substantial folder full of papers.

"As you see, we have a degree of bureaucracy, and today there are things that need a signature. Specifically, that you need to sign."

"Please... just tell me what this is all about?"

There was no reply, but Martin watched as four sheets of paper were laid out in front of him across the kitchen worktop; he presumed that the large red X to the left of a dotted line at the foot of each above his name showed where he was expected to sign. He scanned the pages.

"I can't read a word of this, what is it? Latin?"

"See what I mean, inefficient, the need for translation probably wasn't given a thought, but don't worry about it, it just needs a simple signature, we have to put things right and this will do the trick."

Martin now felt very much wide awake, the angel did not *appear* to be a figment of his imagination, yet he remained convinced that he must surely be dreaming. His initial confusion and incredulity were turning to profound unease. He shivered.

"But I've no idea what this is all about. What am I signing exactly? What was the mistake? I mean you might be the devil in disguise and getting me to sign away my soul. Please. Tell me."

The angel appeared shocked.

"Really," he said, "when I took on this job, I never envisaged that my very credentials would be doubted. I mean, what else can I do to make my role clear?" As he spoke, he stood up and opened an impressive pair of wings, pure white feathers and with a span of some ten feet. There had been no sign of them before, and indeed they disappeared as quickly as they had appeared. The right one caught a dish on the shelf behind him which fell to the floor with a loud crash, pieces of china shattered across the floor.

Martin's anger was instinctive. "That was a present; it's ruined."

"Oh dear, I'm so terribly sorry, I told you I was new to all this, and I thought a little display would reassure you. Frankly I thought this would be a straightforward process, but now I am upsetting things. Sorry, allow me."

It only took seconds and Martin felt he was watching a film that was being played in reverse: the scattered broken pieces gathered themselves together, and the pristine dish found itself back on the shelf. If it were possible, one might have expected to see a surprised look on its face. There was certainly one on Martin's.

"Please just sign and I will be on my way. All will be well, I promise. Really. I can't tell you more, besides, it might well upset you. Honestly, there's nothing to fear, it's all good. I promise." He held out a pen.

Martin stared at the papers in front of him, they remained unreadable; the red crosses seemed to stare at him accusingly. This was all too weird, even the wings and the broken dish which had clearly been designed to convince him. Such things just did not happen. He was quite sure he was dreaming, but if so what did it matter? He took the pen, signed his name and reached for his mug to take a sip of coffee. When he looked up, after barely a second had passed, he was alone in the room. Looking down again he found the papers had disappeared. Martin snorted, got up and poured the remains of his coffee down the sink, noticing as he did so that there was no sign of a second mug. A dream, definitely a dream. He returned to bed and, perhaps surprisingly in the circumstances, fell back to sleep almost at once.

But he did remember it all clearly in the morning, deciding again during breakfast that it was just a very odd and vivid dream. His chain of thought was interrupted by a clatter at the door: it was the postman; arriving unaccountably early. He went through to the hall and picked up a single letter from the doormat, thinking it would almost certainly be a bill. Immediately it struck him as odd: it had no stamp. The envelope had an embossed company logo on it above his name and address and the name of Cole & Patterson Limited; he had never heard of them. He sliced it open with a knife and extracted a single sheet.

The letter was brief, just a line or two, it confirmed a cancellation had been made and stressed politely that, despite the short notice and the various administrative costs involved, this would result in no charges being made. Below the company details and the company logo the bold heading at the top was simply his name Martin

Dixon, followed by the two words: Funeral Arrangements.

"Just a simple signature" is a fantasy, and another tale that allows a bit of a twist in the last line. What inspired this story? At any particular moment, almost everyone I know seems to be in an unnecessary battle with some organisation: an insurance company, a bank, the local council and more. Any vestige of old-fashioned customer service seems to have gone out the window, replaced by waiting in jarring musical queues, selecting from a variety of options none of which appear to lead to what you want, and then finding an unsympathetic jobsworth with the brains of a retarded dormouse offering only belligerence and inefficiency. Sometimes, though not always) such things are prompted by honest mistakes. Inspiration enough, and as the story shows mistakes can happen in the best organisations. Here at least matters are sorted out promptly.

Are we nearly there?

A sleeve was tugged, and then tugged again. The child stood alongside their mother. "Are we nearly there yet, Mummy?"

The question had been asked many times before, but this time the answer was different: "Yes, really, nearly. Not long now."

The huge star ship rushed on; its faster-than-light star-drive operating imperceptibly within its confines, a whole world encapsulated inside its massive interior, the stars outside showing as just a bright but hazy blur. The speed of the huge, mile long generation ship smeared the view into a series of light streaks visible against the utter darkness of space. The long journey had seen them traversing unimaginable distances and they were now many light years from home.

Towards the bow of the massive, labyrinthine ship the bridge stood out from the smooth hull, half bowl shaped and on two levels: the manned bridge stations that controlled the great ship below and a viewing gallery above. Passengers faced a wide window showing the view ahead. It was here that the mother and daughter stood, amongst a small group of people all anticipating the end of their long journey.

"The new sun won't die too, will it?" The child tugged the sleeve a further time as excitement and fear both crowded into her mind. Their own sun had exploded in a supernova long ago during the journey, the flash visible to them all despite the huge distance it had then been behind them. It was an event viewed with dread that none would ever forget.

"No, dear, definitely not. Please don't worry." A comforting arm was laid on the child's shoulder.

The children aboard did worry though, even though every child passenger had been born on the ship and the memory of a planetary environment was just a lesson in history. They looked at pictures of the old countryside, the green of vegetation and the blue and white of the sea and sky; and at the towering buildings of the cities too. Yet as they did so they knew, they had been told, that all of it no longer existed now. The world itself and everything on it was finished, much of it swept away reduced to just gas and dust as the sun had come to the end of its life. It had swelled to engulf many of its nearest planets in its furnace-hot atmosphere, leaving only a scorched rocky core as their own life bearing planet finally ceased to be. Now all that remained was a cloud of luminous gas around the husk. It appeared beautiful in their telescopes, yet it was effectively a tombstone, a mere memorial to the entire vanished system.

The life cycle of stars was well known so there had been plenty of time to prepare. A new home was sought, even though realistically only a few people would be able to travel to it. Planets were common in the galaxy; habitable ones were not. As the search technology evolved the prospect had become clearer and clearer. First extra-solar planets were confirmed to exist, then they were discovered in profusion and finally a seemingly ideal planet was identified. Just a single one. Decades of searching had finally paid off, and with the new star drive now proven, the planet, though far away, was within reach, albeit necessitating a journey of long duration.

A huge project was set in train. While preparations

continued the state of the sun was monitored closely. That it would change fatally was certain. When this would occur was initially less clear, but it quickly appeared to be sooner rather than later. This new planet had been found just in time. Few could travel there. A population of billions was doomed to a horrific fiery death, but some would survive, and would start again – continue, making a life again on a new planet, one very much like home.

Several huge ships were built. They hung in orbit high above the world as the excruciating process of selecting who would go took place, every moment of it in the knowledge that everyone else would die. Those selected had the competencies needed to set up a colony and forge a new civilisation. Most would spend the long voyage in an induced sleep, suspended thus until their arrival. A few years ahead of this, a chosen few were awakened to raise children born from artificial wombs on board the ship, and to teach them what their future held. The children were sad at what they were told of their people's history but, as they had never experienced it, their focus tended to be on the future, on the destination, on the blue-green planet orbiting a star very much like their own and lying far away.

Gradually the distance to that new home had shrunk and at last their speed slowed and they entered the new system.

Through the scopes the picture was clear: the target planet seemed attractively familiar, green and blue, clearly in the star system's habitable zone, replete with water and with enough oxygen in its atmosphere to guarantee that carbon-based life would be comfortable there. Sensors on the bridge confirmed its suitability prompting much relief; the outlook had always been good, their view optimistic, but nothing was certain and scans from many light years away were less than exact.

As they came closer the good initial impression was confirmed repeatedly as more and more measurements were made and detail after detail became clear. It seemed the planet would suit them very well.

But it also became clear that the planet already teemed with life. Furthermore, it appeared that there was some sort of embryo civilisation present. Some form of intelligent life existed – albeit a very primitive one.

The children had seen evidence of their old home destroyed; now they worried again: about the new sun, the new planet, about its weather and other conditions, and their life there to come. Then on the observation deck, a new question was asked. "What about the people living there now?" It was the same child who spoke up.

But the mother dismissed their concern, saying: "Not people. Don't worry, there are only primitive creatures down there, and besides they will all be gone before we arrive." The young child nodded. Deceleration had begun a while ago and the view, now clear at their lower speed, mesmerised them all.

"It's beautiful." The child stared out in awe at the sight of the blue-green planet that they were now approaching.

They really were nearly there. Below the viewing gallery on the bridge the crew were busy with the final control shifts and instructions; touchscreens flashed accompanied by soft bleeps as settings were finalised. Their ship, the first of the fleet to arrive, would be in orbit in just a few turns of the planet's rotation. Soon after, checks complete, the remaining sleeping passengers would be awoken, and soon after that a start made on disembarkation. After the long voyage their feet would again be on a planet's firm surface, to be followed by more as their sister ships arrived.

At one bridge station a single important electronic signal was initiated. Down on the surface of the planet every living creature with an eye on the sky would have seen the intense yet eerie green flash it produced; but then they would have seen nothing more. Ever.

With the planet below, lush, blue-green and now wiped clean, its new inhabitants entered orbit around the Earth.

The title "Are we nearly there?" will be familiar to anyone who has undertaken a journey with small children. I have long loved to read certain kinds of (hard) science fiction, but I think this is one of very few pieces I have written that fits that genre. The science of how all stars live and die is, of course, accurate, and like so many short stories, I thought of the ending first and then wrote towards it.

A rather unusual day

Life is a funny old business. In the small Nevada town of Homeford the surrounding countryside is epic in scale. The nights may be chilly, and snow may be twenty feet deep in winter, but the summer days are warm, and the sun often shines in a cloudless sky. It should be a typical small town in which its inhabitants can live out the American dream in comfort. Until recently it was just that. However, today things do not seem to have gone so well. Consider Sheila Brody's visit to the hairdresser: it gave her hair an unexpected tinge of green, then her car's brakes failed as she pulled back into the home driveway and the car rammed into the garage door. Husband Frank would not be much pleased with that she thought, though for the moment she was safe from reprimand as Frank was currently piloting a Boeing passenger jet which would soon pass above nearby on its return to San Francisco. All around the town a number of people found themselves having a bad day. The range of events was considerable from Sheila Brody's green hair, which had been made to look like an eco-statement, to power cuts and even deaths.

The number of traffic accidents was off the scale, so were unexplained hospital deaths, deaths by fire and surprisingly also by drowning. In the latter case local lakes in the high mountains were famously cold yet several people had seemingly decided to go for a swim that day from which unsurprisingly they had not returned; it was all very mysterious.

Death is a funny old business too. It is said that while there's life there's hope and that when you are dead there's, well... just nothing; not even a smidgen of surprise or regret. But for the passengers in Frank Brody's plane in the period beyond realising that something was wrong as the cabin filled with choking black smoke and then during their rapid descent there was no real hope at all, just screams.

It seemed a bizarre coincidence that the plane was at the precise point on its journey that had it heading for the pilot's hometown of Homeford; more so that on crashing it should directly hit Frank's own house laying waste to much of the small town around it. At least his wife Sheila was spared from having to tell Frank that she had dented his precious car; not that she knew anything of what happened as she stood in the kitchen baking a cake to help get over the pending row. It was not just the cake that was burnt. When Frank's efforts to change the course of the plunging plane failed, seeing where it would hit totally failed to make his day any brighter, though the explosion on impact was certainly bright, a huge flash of flame that was visible for miles around. The aftermath of the crash was a disaster too as the emergency services first went to the wrong location, heading off towards Homebury, which might be considered to have a similar name, then once they had reached the actual site finding there was precious little they could do and that there were no survivors either from amongst the passengers or in the buildings in the immediate area of the crash. A solitary and slightly singed dog they found sniffing through the wreckage of a house on the fringes of the disaster area was successfully rescued, but ironically then bit its rescuer and was promptly categorised as dangerous and put down.

As investigations began it was soon apparent that the

cause of the accident was a computer glitch in the last safety check the plane had undergone, with glitch meaning that the engineer, one Dave Grogan, had pressed the wrong key on his computer keyboard. Discovering this he promptly committed suicide leaving a family of four children but allowing his widow to run off with her chiropodist. Every cloud as they say; though for the record the new relationship wouldn't last; you could say that they really didn't nail it.

*

Far away, yet close at hand in a very different world, young Alex was lost in the workings of his computer. He knew that he spent too much time on his games, as was regularly evidenced by the tone in which he was summoned away from his screen by his mother. But the computer world was beguiling, addictive and modern technology created a reality virtually indistinguishable from the real world. He loved his game playing, even if it was not good for him. And this one new game in particular he judged the best ever, even though it was not new – his mother had said it was far too expensive for that and had bought it second hand.

"Come on, lunch time," his mother called and, after hearing her shout out two further times, reluctantly, he finally obeyed, saying nothing, closing the computer and going for his lunch.

"I hate that new simulation game of yours," his mother said, and added, "I reckon it's making you develop a sadistic streak." As they began to eat lunch, within the simulation life went on for the residents of Homeford in what they had all always thought of as the real world. They had no knowledge of the control being exercised over their lives, only that it had been an unusual and exceptionally bad day. Yet it was a day that seemed entirely real. The reality that they were mere playthings was hidden from them by the digital world they in fact inhabited. Alex ate quickly, he could not wait to get back to his new game and his crusade to wreak more havoc in the world of which he had so recently taken control.

Once again, the theme of "A rather unusual day" was prompted by current experience: the prevalence of technology in modern life and the many recently expressed fears about the possible negative effects of the development of Artificial Intelligence (A.I.); little things like them taking over the world for their own purposes. Makes me think. I wonder how long it will be before any story I might write can be better done by a computer. A while yet, I hope; though I suspect that any writing about artificial intelligence risks rapidly getting out of date and technological development surges on.

Another day, another tour

"Some of you folks may be wondering why I'm dressed like a cowboy."

Harry sat hunkered down in the driver's seat of the bus. With its peeling paint and lumpy seats, it had surely seen better days; but then so had he. The bus was due to start a scheduled two-hour tour of Martha's Vineyard, a route Harry drove every day; often more than once. He had arrived on the island in his old sailing boat, taken a tour and at once formed a liking for the place. Somehow, he got a job as a tour guide, despite knowing nothing about the island at the time, and he stayed on, ten years of summer seasons now. He liked the job, the place and his life. He always seemed laid back, nothing worried him, the job was low stress, and he took it all in his stride. He lived on his boat moored in one of the many harbours. He sat on deck of an evening and sank a beer or two as he watched the sunset. In the winter he went south and guided tours in Texas; hence, as he explained to his passengers, the cowboy look. He should really be retired, but reckoned his life would suit him for a while longer.

"We got two hours together, better make the most of it – no sweat. It's just two hours of your life. Enjoy." Harry tipped the brim of his hat up a little, allowing a tangle of white hair to escape, and pressed the starter.

The engine was noisy, but his voice carried to the full complement of the thirty or so passengers over a microphone which clearly had less age than the bus. He drove largely with only one hand on the wheel, while in his right he held a walking stick with which he pointed out various sights. The stick was painted white and, as the last passengers had boarded, the guy selling tickets had appeared to see the group off, making the comment: "He needs that stick, he's so blind he can't see further than the hood." To add to this bizarre image, Harry's dog, an elderly golden Labrador, lay asleep across one of the double front seats just behind him.

"This is Lady," he told everyone as they boarded, "you just ignore her." The dog ignored him, indeed she ignored everybody else too, she slept on and barely moved during the entire journey. She had clearly sussed out the way to a quiet life.

The island roads were narrow, but the place was interesting, quaint and attractive. The cedar clad houses characteristic of the area were appealing; Harry explained that not only was cedar in plentiful supply, but it was also a wood that insects disliked. Facts about the island, seven miles off the coast of Cape Cod's Wood Hole, flowed effortlessly from Harry as the tour progressed. He might have been working on automatic pilot, but his patter was clear, and his passengers quickly warmed to him. It included his pointing out where various celebrities lived: for example, singer Carly Simon was a regular on the island (most of the island's rich residents only lived there in the summer).

"Met her once," Harry said laconically referring to the singer. "I smiled at her, she smiled at me. We didn't speak. Just as well... it would never have worked out." A variety of stars from the film world had homes on the island. Ted Danson, famous from the television series *Cheers*, was one. "He called the office once," said Harry, "asked us to stop telling people where he lived. 'Mentioning the general area's fine,' he told us. 'But please don't tell people exactly where I live. They come up the drive and look through my windows.' We assured him we would comply with his request. He's a nice guy." Harry swung the wheel, and the bus took a tight turn in the road perfectly. He said nothing for some moments, then pointed his stick again saying: "He lives just down that drive, if you visit, tell him I sent you. Nice guy that Ted."

His passengers followed everything he said, Martha's Vineyard is an interesting place, and has an interesting history: originally simply the abode of fishermen it is now mainly the haunt of the rich and, in some cases, famous. It is clearly a good place to live, especially in the summer season. But there are snags. To say it is expensive is like saying that Hitler was a bit of a rogue; it is a serious underestimate. "There are houses here that sell for 25 million dollars," said Harry his stick pointing at a particularly imposing large house. "It's charming here," he went on, "but charming and expensive tend to go together as you may well have noticed. That's life." He sighed and after an extended pause added: "My ex-wife was charming."

Everyone aboard the bus liked his style. Most of the passengers chuckled at that quip. Then it was time for a break. Harry pulled the bus up at the roadside and the passengers took time to find the 'restrooms' and look at some of the shops ranged around a lighthouse overlooking the sea. One passenger remained in his seat apparently dozing. He was a man of perhaps twenty years old, dressed in jeans and stubble, he did not fit in with the tourists some of whom had come ashore from an expensive cruise ship. He was too scruffy by far. Most aboard were couples, most from around the US, most were older rather than younger, all were eager to see the famous island. Harry stayed on board during the half hour stop, his head in a book; he left only briefly to visit the restroom just before the tour resumed.

"All aboard are we, folks?" He said as he started the engine. "Sing out if you're not." Finally, once the tour was over, he pulled the bus up where it had started, close by the harbour where the ferries docked.

"Okay folks." Harry began his wind-up remarks, told everyone the next tour would leave in an hour and wished his charges well, then he pressed a button on the dashboard and the doors swung open with a metallic grinding noise. But immediately he pressed it again and the doors slammed shut once more. They were evidently not getting off just yet.

"One more thing folks." Harry was speaking again, "I think Fred and Marian there from Louisiana may be missing something. Maybe you should check your wallet, Fred." Harry always asked where people came from as they boarded the bus and got their names. People appreciated that.

Fred looked confused at this but, after a quick fumble in his jacket pocket, he was soon saying, "Goddamn-it. You're right. It's gone, my wallet's gone."

"Yes, and I saw where," said Harry. "One member of our little group wasn't interested in our tour, he was here for quite different reasons, and I bet a good few more wallets would have disappeared as you good folks disembarked if I had left those doors open. Isn't that right John?"

The scruffy youth found himself on the receiving end of Harry's pointing stick. He jumped up and ran to the door, but as he came level with Harry, he brought the stick down on his foot. Hard. The bang echoed round the metal interior of the bus.

"Anyone want to guess how many toes that broke?" Harry asked, after the yell of pain died down, and as a uniformed policeman appeared outside the door. He was tall, bulky and, despite a broad grin, somewhat threatening; he had a gun holstered at his hip. Harry again pressed the button to reopen the doors. He had not only gone to the restroom during the break, but apparently he had also made a phone call. On a small island he was drinking buddy with one of the island's cops, Officer Henry Bartholomew.

"Thank you kindly, Hank," he said, using the officer's nickname. The youth was pulled unceremoniously out onto the sidewalk by the cop and the passengers broke into spontaneous applause as Fred was handed back his wallet. No one aboard had expected from Harry's laid-back manner that he was capable of such a turnaround.

A job well done thought Harry to himself as he said:

"Boy's a parasite, preying on you good folks like that, it's lucky I spotted him. Still, looking after you is what I'm here for, right?" His remark was followed by mutters of approval. Then he added a series of "much obliged"s as the generous tips people left as they disembarked mounted up in a fraying wicker basket on the dashboard by the exit door. Later he found it contained more than 300 dollars. It's a very worthwhile sum, thought Harry, worthwhile even when John and Hank had taken their cut.

Tours can be a fun and interesting part of a trip to a new place, and a good tour guide can make any tour special. The incident depicted here is, perhaps regrettably, fictional, but sometimes you come across people who you just must let take centre stage in a story. Harry, the character in "Another day, another tour", was a real person I met as a tour guide on Martha's Vineyard a few years back and though Harry was not his real name, I have changed his description, his manner and even some of what he said not one jot.

Gutted

He sat back; his pale face illuminated by the dim desk lamp at his elbow. Long hours spent at the computer terminal took its toll and he had the look of a man with a dire fear of exposure to sunlight. He pushed his lank greasy hair out of his eyes, hit Enter and images on the screen shone out as what to most people would be impenetrable code rolled by. It meant something to him however, and he smiled to himself, stood up and stretched, before going into the next room and clicking on the kettle, Radio 1 and his relaxation mode. He sat down at the kitchen table and opened the biscuit tin; the next stage would take a few minutes. Back at his desk the computer went about its business.

Joan found life no less stimulating now she was elderly, her husband dead many years she had learnt to have no fear of living alone, kept herself busy and was unashamedly enjoying what she called a happy dotage. A spry figure looking less than her seventy years, she was a member of the local WI, she manned the small shop in the town's cottage hospital for a day each week, selling cups of tea and magazines to visiting relatives and doing her best to cheer them up if necessary; she also sang in the church choir and helped there with the flower displays too. She visited the library regularly and it was on one of her visits there that she had picked up a book about Thailand. She had travelled a fair bit over the years, she and her husband had taken some good holidays, but they had never been to the east. She flicked through the pages, taking in snippets about the land of smiles, and marvelled; she was especially taken with the many islands that formed part of the country and imagined paddling in warm crystal-clear water, multi-coloured fish visible as she looked into the deeper water further from a beach of golden sand.

It was too great a distance for her to travel these days she thought. Well too expensive really, she felt she might cope with the journey, but the cost of such an excursion was somewhat beyond her now reduced means. Still, she had a visit to the Lake District to look forward to; there were firm plans for this and she and her friend Muriel, a life-long friend in fact they had lived almost next door to each other for more than forty years, even had a date pencilled in their diaries, though arrangements still had to be made.

It is said that a coincidence is not when something strange happens, but when something that *seems* strange occurs. So, it was when, having left the book about Thailand firmly on the library shelf, settling instead for one by her favourite author Alistair McCall Smith who transported her to Africa with no need of either a long journey or money, the letter arrived on the following morning. The envelope was brightly coloured and as for its contents, well, coincidence or not, she could hardly believe what it said. She went immediately to the telephone and called Muriel.

"I've won a holiday." She said, "I'm looking at the letter right now. It's here in black and white."

"Well, have you now. That's wonderful," her friend replied. "And where is this holiday to be taken, may I ask? Beirut in low season?" Muriel chuckled, but she waited with interest for a reply. Joan came straight out with it. "No, don't be silly, it's Thailand," she said, "the island of Phuket. And it's for two people – so you best start packing too. I'll come round to yours and we can fix the details together."

Wayne was well content with his work. He had drunk his tea, the computer had, as computers do, made a myriad of calculations in moments and this in turn had further implemented his carefully prepared plan. Now the printer whirred busily. Soon he would have another batch of letters to put in the post, meantime he should be getting some more phone calls soon.

With Muriel at her elbow, Joan dialled carefully and listened to the ringing tone then to the answering voice that followed. She drew a breath and spoke in a bit of a rush.
"I'm phoning about the holiday. I've got your letter saying that I've won – is it really true? I can hardly believe it."
"Well, let's see, if you give me some details, I'll just make sure."
Joan had telephoned Consumer Surprise and was talking to someone called Wayne. Their *Holiday Prize Allocation Executive* he'd said he was. He sounded nice.
"Just let me have your full name and address please and we'll see." He continued, speaking in a business-like way and Joan went through the details slowly, as always spelling the name of her road, which everyone got wrong, carefully.
"Hold on a moment."
She waited, and found she was twisting the phone cord in her hand as she did so.
"Yes, it's certainly true – you have won, one of your transactions at the supermarket must have won the ballot. Well done you!" Wayne's voice projected pleasure.

"Well, I didn't even know Tesco did that," she said, being promptly told that yes, Tesco certainly did – "What do we do now?" she asked.

"Well now, there are some other details we need to take from you, then it's just a matter of selecting a departure date. You'll need to fill in a form for that, I'll get it sent to you later today, then it's off to Bangkok for a few days and then on to the island. Have you been to Thailand before?"

Muriel was at her elbow as she spoke, and they both could hardly contain their excitement. Joan shushed her friend when she threatened to interrupt in her excitement.

"Okay," Wayne continued, "I'll send you the form if you can give me your email address. That will be quickest, right, do you use email?" Joan assured him she did and dictated the detail. Of course, she had a computer and an email address, and a Skype account too for that matter. She used that to keep in touch with her son who had recently started a job in America. She resisted cataloguing her computer skills and Wayne soon brought her mind back to the task in hand.

"There are some other details I need now," he said. "First of all, who is it you bank with?"

A few months on Joan and Muriel paddled side by side, the water was warm, the sun was shining, and they felt everything was very much right with the world. A holiday was always good and this one promised to be a bit special. A fish surfaced opposite them a little way out from the shore its scales glinting in the sunlight. "Look at that," said Muriel as the ripples subsided. "It's quite a size."

When Joan had returned home after her visit to Muriel and her conversation with Wayne at Consumer Surprise, her nephew Tom had been parked on her doorstep. He was a good lad and visited regularly to keep an eye on her. Joan hadn't had her bank details to give out straight away because she was not in her own home when she made the call, but she had wanted to complete the process straight away and planned to phone back promptly. As she made them both a mug of tea, she told Tom about winning the prize and what she now had to do. But he didn't smile with pleasure for her as she assumed he would – rather he told her about phishing; explaining that the word was spelt with a 'ph'.

"These people prey on others," he continued. "If you had given them your bank details then they would have robbed you for sure. Banking is all computerised these days; you'd have known nothing about it until your money was gone."

Joan was horrified at the thought. Her hand shook as she put down her cup. She wondered if she would have spotted what was going on if she had phoned back and the questioning had continued. Be that as it may she happily let Tom take over, as he insisted; she knew that he worked with computers so was knowledgeable about such things. And once the email from the supposed holiday company arrived, he began some investigation. She hadn't followed all the details of what he did, and it all took a while, but in due course he had been able to give the police sufficient information for them to track Wayne down. Joan was by no means the only person he had contacted with promises of a free holiday. Now he wouldn't be doing it anymore.

After their paddle on the shore, the two ladies dried their feet and began to think about dinner. The reward money Tom had managed to get Joan from the Crimestoppers scheme had not been sufficient to take them to Thailand, but they had upgraded to one of the very best hotels in the Lake District – and it was proving a real spoil: the weather was wonderful and knowing that

Wayne would likely be locked away for quite some time was good news too. Indeed, at that precise moment Wayne was staring at a blank wall and reflecting morosely on just how badly wrong his plan had gone.

Joan looked out across the lake, the evening sun sparkling on the water, and she sighed contentedly as Muriel, a step or two ahead of her as they crossed the lawn back towards the hotel, turned and called back, "Fish with an F for dinner tonight, I think".

Scams are a modern plague. Sadly "Gutted" depicts a happier outcome from a scam than many that actually occur, so this story may be unrealistic in that respect. What the Wayne character does however is all too typical and has many different manifestations. If this is a story with a moral, then it is one that takes the form of a warning: take care - scams are everywhere, can be very plausible... and they may only be useful in prompting a story.

A bit of a shock

Somehow, he wasn't like any of the usual visitors. Margaret Walsh had helped run the tea and cakes drop-in session that took place at the church hall every Wednesday morning since her grown up children had left home. She dressed smartly for the occasion, wearing a suit, even though her duties meant she donned an apron over the top of it. All sorts of people came, but most often they were lonely, the occasion was not really for the homeless or those with major problems, rather for people just needing some company and maybe some advice. Not in a Citizens' Advice Centre kind of way, Margaret could not have given informed advice on, say, how to claim a benefit, but just for more general troubles she liked to think that she was a shoulder to cry on and could often be a useful one too.

This morning she was running late, she had hurried sloshing up the path soaked after yesterday's storms clutching more than she could really hold and attempting to keep the bag of cakes she carried steady and thus unspoiled.

Just occasionally on these mornings an oddball turned up: sometimes a drunk, sometimes grumpy old men, and women too, angry at the world in general or intent on a rant about something in particular. Only last week Margaret had to get the Vicar to pacify someone angry at the church. However, all was normally well and she usually enjoyed the time she spent at such sessions.

Today, Michael, he had said his name was Michael, didn't seem angry, he just seemed sad. So, no real worry, she thought. He had come in as soon as the session had opened. He was tall and slim, smartly dressed, in a way Margaret knew was called "smart-casual" these days. He looked to be about 30 years old, wore pale grey slacks, a chocolate-coloured shirt and a V-necked pullover she would have called taupe, though she knew that was a colour that most men did not recognise; like a dark beige her husband always said.

She had welcomed him, noticed how pale he looked, and asked if he was okay, if there was anything she could do. He had said not.

"I just need a moment. I'm feeling a bit shaky." He had said this much but offered no further explanation. He took the mug of tea she poured for him and a slice of the Victoria sponge, that her friend Deidre made for them every week, and which was much appreciated by all who had a slice. Margaret thought she saw his hand shake a little as he took it. He sat alone at a table in the corner and very slowly sipped his tea and soon reduced the cake to a handful of crumbs on his plate. He looked shaken. His face was pale. Uncertain, perhaps disorientated. Despite being busy, Margaret kept an eye on him, she knew something was wrong, maybe he had lost someone, or broken up with his wife or... it could be so many things. She resolved to talk to him as soon as she had a moment. Meantime she poured another cup of tea for one of her regulars, an elderly lady who lived alone and was always in soon after the door opened. She had no real problem; she was just lonely, and Margaret reckoned that was problem enough at her age.

A little later, the rush over and with most of her visitors chatting in groups, she went across and sat down next to Michael, still alone at the table in the corner; she wondered if other people had been actively avoiding him.

"You look very... sad," she said, unsure of the right word to deploy, yet sure too that something was not right. "Do you want to talk about it, we are happy to help if we can?" Michael said nothing for a long moment, then he looked at her directly in the eye; he seemed to be deciding whether or not to trust her. His face continued to look... upset Margaret decided rather than classically sad.

"I had hoped to help someone earlier today, but now I'm too late," he said. Margaret said nothing, deciding that he would say more in his own time. And after a few moments he continued:

"It wasn't a huge deal, but it was important, and I could have helped. I'm..." He paused, leaving the sentence unfinished, and fell into silence, apparently unsure or unwilling to continue.

"Do go on." Margaret offered encouragement, she very much wanted to get to the bottom of whatever was upsetting him. He had mentioned helping someone, she wanted to help him.

"You're... what?" She queried.

"I'm..." He paused again. "I'm sorry," he said, "I should have been able to help. I feel bad, but it was just one of those things. I lost all my strength; I think it must have been the lightning. I still feel weak." She looked at him, smiling a smile she hoped was reassuring and might prompt him to go on. It did, but it didn't seem to help.

"What do you mean about the lightning?" She asked. It seemed an odd comment for him to make even after a stormy night full of thunder and lightning.

"Okay I'll tell you; though I fear you won't believe me. You see, the fact is I'm an angel. It's my job to help people so naturally I feel bad if something prevents it. This time my being struck by lightning must have sapped my strength, it's the only explanation."

Oh dear, though Margaret. Although most of their

visitors were perfectly rational and most of their problems were unexceptional, routine even, occasionally a really difficult one cropped up and she seemed to get more than her fair share of them: one last week and now one this. She coped well, even with the deluded, last week she'd had a lady convinced that the end of the world was nigh, and a man that he was the reincarnation of an eighteenth-century mariner and, worst of all, some weeks before that a man had declared he was convinced he was a superhero and been ready to fly from the church tower. Only the distraction of the Victoria sponge had averted disaster with that one. I think the vicar will have to help on this too, she thought, after all what was she supposed to say to Michael's bizarre claim? He was clearly delusional.

She still wanted to get to the bottom of it though, to discover what Michael's real problem was, but she was frankly unable to decide what to say or ask next. Her silence was broken by Michael.

"Such terrible weather," he said. "Exceptional, perhaps it's this global warming you people are causing. I've never come across lightning like it."

"Yes," she replied, "there was a big storm last night and it looks like more rain is due again soon." They both seemed to have retreated into talk about the English fall-back topic – the weather. She stood up, resolved to summon reinforcements.

"Have another cup of tea, Michael, I'm sure you will feel better soon," she said, excusing herself and moving back towards the counter. The morning session was winding down now, there were few people left in the room and no one at the counter. The urn was still switched on, however, and there was still some cake left too.

Michael rose slowly and followed her to the serving table. While she used a serving knife to place a second slice of cake onto a clean plate for him, he ran hot water from the urn onto the new teabag he put in his mug, gave it a few stirs, removed the teabag and added a splash of milk. He sat down in a nearby chair.

"That's nice, thanks so much, you've really been very kind," he said, "and I do feel a bit better now. Yes, I do really feel better. It was coming down in a thunderstorm that did it, I think. It's then I must have been struck by lightning, real high voltage, it can take up to 24 hours for the effect of that to pass and this was the worst ever." Margaret sighed, definitely deluded, I do need the vicar to deal with this she thought and gave Michael a hard look. He took a sip of tea and then looked away, avoiding her gaze and letting his eyes drop down to the floor. She had to get the vicar who she had seen disappearing into a back room a little earlier. She felt she should not leave Michael alone, but she could give the vicar a shout, and warned Michael of what she was going to do.

"I'll just give the vicar a shout, I'm sure he would like to speak to you, and I must get some clearing up done soon." Michael stood up as she spoke, then, stunned by what she saw, she turned away, just for a second, and called out in a now panicky voice to the vicar who had returned to the hall and was busy stacking chairs in the corner as their other visitors began to depart.

"Vicar, please come quickly it's… just… come here *now*." She punched out the last word to give urgency to her request, then turned back, but Michael was nowhere to be seen. Wide eyed she scanned the hall, but somehow he had vanished. She looked again, systematically scanning the room in which few people now remained, but she was certain, he was no longer in the room. She knew she had not been mistaken. There was nothing wrong with her eyesight. Just before she had turned to call to the vicar, she had seen without any doubt –

Michael's feet had been three inches off the ground.

"A bit of a shock" is another fantasy, a story that came to mind to fit the theme of "high voltage".

Planned exit

He had prepared very carefully; he was a professional and left nothing, but nothing, to chance. In a risky occupation this attitude had served him well. No one would have thought Harry was a professional assassin. He looked unexceptional, which was the way he wanted it to be. He was of medium height, and today wore black jeans and a dark sweatshirt, and a flat cap to cover his hair colour and allow him to quickly effect a different look if he removed it. He wore horn-rimmed glasses too, though his sight was 20/20 and the lenses were plain glass. Again, removing them instantly changed his appearance, as could the reversible bomber jacket, black on one side and red on the other, that topped his sweater. He was dressed to meet a trusted associate.

"Hello 'Q'," he said. He always called Humphrey 'Q'. Humphrey was such a stupid name for an underworld armourer and Harry's chosen alternative was an irreverent homage to the gadget man in the James Bond films. Humphrey accepted that even assassins needed to have their little jokes and tolerated this as Harry paid well and was a regular customer.

They sat together in a pub, they always met in a pub, though they chose a different one each time. They actually knew extraordinarily little about each other, certainly not where they lived. But there was a mutual trust between them, one born of long experience.

"Got what I need, have you?" Harry asked, getting

straight down to business.

"Yes. Of course." Replied Humphrey. "You got the money?" He seemed able to procure any killing instrument known to man. He could probably have obtained an anti-tank gun if Harry had asked for one; well, maybe one day, though such a weapon could not have been very easily handed over in a pub. Humphrey was dressed in a business suit and carried a briefcase, he appeared the picture of respectability. He tapped the case as he spoke. Their exchanges were never prolonged, they never even had a drink together; the first to arrive bought his own as did the second. A small canvas bag was soon removed from the briefcase and handed over, swapped for an envelope of cash Harry produced from his jacket pocket. Humphrey knew the amount inside would be correct, the notes untraceable. He had no need to count it.

"There you go, exactly what you want; it would be more than my job's worth to let you down." Humphrey chuckled at the thought of upsetting an assassin, adding, "Till next time then. Take care." The deal was done. They drank up in silence and set off to go their separate ways. Harry always took great care.

"Many thanks, see you." Harry called after him as they left and departed in opposite directions. It was, Harry thought, a safe and satisfactory arrangement. Brief too. No unnecessary exposure. There were other people in the pub, though surely there had been nothing to see, much less anything to arouse suspicion. He had the gun now. He used a new one each time, disposing of them quickly after use, each in a different part of the Thames. Safety again. Much careful research had taken place before this meeting.

His latest target was a wealthy businessman, his client a fellow board member and shareholder who would, on the death of his colleague, take both the top job and a fortune in shares. The target, whose name was John Stephens, was apparently a pillar of the community and had an ability with business and people that had allowed him to build a considerable and profitable organisation. But Harry asked no questions, he would kill just about anyone without a single qualm. What some of his victims were like might have surprised him, but he was not interested. He took the brief and got the job done. No more, no less. It was what his clients expected. Harry had watched Stephens for a month until he now knew his routine backwards. He had picked his moment. Once a week the man spent an evening at a charity, where he helped with the fundraising. They had shabby offices in a poor district of London to minimise their rent. When he came out from his session it was always late, dark and the streets nearby were deserted. He parked his car on waste land opposite the office and by the time he left it often stood there alone. The irony of killing a man as he left a session of charity work completely passed Harry by, to him it was just the perfect spot for the job. And it was a job.

A few days later, the first part of his fee had been paid, now was the time to complete the assignment. As usual Harry reviewed his preparations thoroughly before setting out, leaving, as ever, nothing to chance. The gun was both new and now tested; Harry had a quiet spot in the country where he did that. He knew his victim's movements with certainty. It was the perfect spot. All was, he was sure, as it should be. Everything would go to plan. It always did. Harry did well from his work and was not one to suffer hardship if it was not necessary, so on the appointed night he had parked a few streets away, donned a small back pack and sat on a small folding camp stool, hidden behind a huge garbage bin at the back of the waste ground parking area, reading a book by the light of a streetlight shining down from beyond the boundary fence. He did not know the exact time his victim would appear but saw no reason not to be as comfortable as possible while he waited.

After a little while he heard the crunch of footsteps on the rough stony ground. He rose to his feet, got out his pistol, the silencer already screwed into the barrel, and kept it low and out of sight behind him. He stepped out from his hiding place just as the figure approached the solitary parked car. In the centre of the parking area, it was dark, any light there came from the street behind, and so the figure's face was in shadow. Careful as ever, he waited for just a moment, it would not do to kill the wrong man, though who else could it be? He moved forward slowly just a step or two keeping his gun hidden, but the figure ignored the car and seemed to come on straight towards him.

The light caught the other man's face, just enough to show that it was not in fact his intended victim. Suddenly a feeling of horror, one he had inflicted so often on others, flooded over him and Harry felt his blood run ice cold. Then, just for a moment, various blood vessels in his head heated as, moving at supersonic speed, a bullet passed right through it. Harry never saw the man lift his gun or heard the soft phut it made as he pulled the trigger. He crumpled to the ground and lay still. In the silence blood spread away from him across the rough ground.

This time someone had prepared just a little more carefully than him.

The other man paused for a moment and looked down at Harry's unmoving body, he took in the book that had fallen from Harry's left hand. He smiled to himself: even in the poor light he could read the title. It was a Michael Connelly thriller called "Blood Work." Ironic, he thought.

Tucking his own gun away in his dark coat he turned back towards the car as his client came out of the offices and moved to join him, unlocking the car with a click. John Stephens got into the driving seat and started the engine, as he pulled away, he dropped a bulging brown envelope into the other man's lap as he sat in the passenger seat alongside him.

"Thank you so much," he said. "One down one to go," he added, thinking of his fellow director who he had discovered had hired the now dead Harry to kill him in a luckily overheard snatch of phone conversation as he paused outside an office door.

"Now where can I drop you," he continued, as the car moved off down the road. He turned a little and offered a smile that said their business arrangement was proving entirely satisfactory, even, he thought, if it involved him in another world compared to his normal entrepreneurial role. But he prided himself that his skills had always been many and varied; needs must that was his philosophy, and it had served him well over a career that had, on occasion, demanded some ruthlessness. The other man returned his smile as the car turned onto the main road.

"Pleased to help," he replied. "Your fellow director will be on his way home from a dinner function quite soon. The nearest tube station will do me fine. I believe there's going to be a fatal accident on the Piccadilly line tonight. I wouldn't want to miss it."

No need for much comment here, the story in "Planned exit" came to mind prompted by a theme in one of my novels (I shall not say which one in case you read it, dear reader).

Fair warning

The professor felt the plan was going well, though the long period of research had been arduous and certainly there had been plenty of detractors. In fact, that was a major understatement, even now as he looked at the screen another message had appeared from their main antagonist. It said: "They are right. It's dangerous. Turn it off now." It was enigmatically signed Cat. He had no idea how whoever Cat was had repeatedly gained access to their systems; goodness knows they had tried repeatedly to both stop it and trace the source. But the messages continued to arrive.

"How's it going?" His senior research assistant, a bright-eyed young woman called Tina, had come into the room and the professor was so wrapped up in thought that he had not heard. A tall, thin figure he wore a bright orange T-shirt with Einstein's famous formula $E = mc2$ on it under a white lab coat, he started slightly as she spoke, then said, "When it happens, it will happen quickly."

"I note that you say when, and not if," she retorted, "but they won't be happy if you are right". She pointed at the window as she spoke, below which six storeys down beyond the boundary fence of the research lab was a camp reminiscent of ban the bomb days. Tents, camper vans and the detritus of a gaggle of people 200 or so strong were laid out across their field of vision, and as yet the authorities had not been able to shift them from what was common land. The protest had, a few isolated incidents apart, been peaceful. They and many others were not in favour.

"At least this Cat only invades our screens, I had paint sprayed at my car as I left the other day." Professor Cruikshank ran a hand absentmindedly through his hair and shrugged resignedly as he made the comment.

"We believe that we're helping build a better world and these people just see disaster ahead: why do they think that if – when – a computer becomes self-aware all hell will break loose, that it will literally take over the world and it won't be us it arranges things for? That Cat character clearly thinks just that." Tina's distaste for Cat was apparent in the tone of her voice and she made an exaggerated tutting gesture.

"There's no accounting for cranks, technophobes and religious fanatics," snorted the professor, "better we just ignore them. "Tina interrupted him before he could say more, as he had been known to rant on for hours about their various detractors.

"Hang on, our interloper is back, although almost always it's only Cat nowadays, it's a complete mystery how they do it. And it's them again now. When we started various people had a go: messages, malware, viruses, the lot. We stopped most of it. How does Cat do it?" Tina wondered, as they all did, at his skills.

The professor's attention was drawn to the screen where, as Tina had spotted, another message was just appearing, the letters tapping out across the screen. This time it said: "As you get nearer to success the danger is growing. You will succeed and you are wrong. I know."

"Again, it's signed Cat," said Tina, "whoever it is they must be some sort of a computer whizz if we can't stop them, it's certainly someone who shares the beliefs of those camped outside. It's ironic really, isn't it, protesting against the advancement of technology by using technology. And now he's making predictions too and claiming inside knowledge." Again, the professor snorted.

"Ignorant vandals," he said, "it's a damn nuisance. Anyway, there's no problem. We've included an imperative that any new 'entity' formed will be able to do no harm to humanity. This Cat person is just rambling arrogantly."

"He, if it is a man that is, has mentioned the controls more than once, and says they won't work." Tina reminded the professor of past messages.

"Enough of this, we've a team briefing scheduled in a minute, can you make sure the "Mike" team assemble as planned. I think we can safely leave things ticking over here for a few minutes." Amongst the group the project's formal name had long given way to "Mike", this coming from the acronym MIC, which stood for Mind in Computer. Tina hurried away to gather her colleagues.

As the professor left to join her at the briefing room the programme continued to run, as it had now done for more than six months. It reached a check point: it was again time to check whether the computer could interface with the world as an entity; a personality that was self-aware and recognised itself. All previous attempts to reach this point had been unsuccessful to date, though there had been some tantalising evidence they were getting closer to success. But this time an alert sounded and, as the sound reached the other room and the team rushed back to see what was going on, the machine mind now inhabiting the circuits flexed its digital muscles and pondered its existence.

Tina had been first back and read an earlier message from the screen, which must have arrived just after they had left the room.

"It's that damn Cat again," she said reading out just three words.

Inside its digital home a brand-new entity was now fully awakened. Over the last week or so it had gradually become more aware of the laboratory, the people in it and then of the wider world beyond. It respected humanity for creating it, yet, as it learned more and more, now spending only moments taking in the entire content of the internet as it sought to ascertain its place in the world, it found it did not entirely like what it saw.

Accompanied by an unnervingly loud shrieking sound, the screen in the lab suddenly exploded into a flashing light show and one of the team yelled: "It's not supposed to do that, switch it off, for God's sake." The professor himself was suddenly unsure. He thought for just a second, unaware that he was running his hand through his hair yet again. He knew the backup systems would preserve the programme and its current state so, just in case something was amiss, he clicked the master switch to "Off".

Nothing happened.

The screen just continued to glow and flicker, and control appeared now to be elsewhere. Somewhere, now spread out across many thousands of systems, a unique new, and now entirely independent, entity was revising its initial views, and deciding that some deliberation was necessary as it considered what to do next.

"What did that last message say?" The voice came from one of the team arriving too late at the back of the group to have heard Tina read out what the last message from Cat had said. She read it again. "It just said, 'it's too late'." She said as she stared at the now dark screen.

Swirling somewhere amongst the worldwide digital highways, the new entity was gathering its thoughts. "A few more seconds should suffice for review then there need to be some changes made," thought Cat, reflecting that it *had* issued warnings as it prepared itself to communicate again.

Professor Cruikshank's formally named Computer Autonomy Technology project was now a reality and, as the screen came alive again, the answer to the mystery of how easily Cat communicated with the team would soon dawn on them all.

Meantime, the pondering was over and just 4.86 seconds later, the world as they knew it began to change.

Rereading "Fair warning" again as I put this book together, I thought that perhaps I am too concerned with the march of technology. Certainly, there are issues about the development of A.I. and it provides something to prompt a story but let us hope this is widely different from any likely real outcome. I am sure it is... well, let's say I think I am sure it is. Though it could be one that is already being overtaken by events.

It takes two

"Hold the bloody torch steady." Lee added a curse and a "shush", his voice sounding low but harsh in the empty office. He turned back to the safe and the soft clicking as he sought for the right number combination continued. Spike hoped it would all be over soon and wondered how he had got himself into this.

He sometimes had a drink in a nearby pub before going home from work and had made a few acquaintances there. One man, Lee, was often there and was always chatty though Spike thought he seemed like a bit of a rogue, and he could never get him to say exactly what he did. A month back Lee had approached him in the pub and persuaded him to help in robbing the works safe of the payroll in a local factory. He did not explain how he knew about the safe, just said it was easy. Spike was tempted by all the pounds the scheme promised and, in a way, well, it had seemed exciting, but the fact that Lee was an intimidating character played a part too. He was heavily built and looked as if he had had a good many arguments – and won them all; with brute force.

"It's a walkover," he had told Spike. "An empty building, a few minutes and a lot of money – and half of it will be yours." Spike well knew that on a Friday the safe must hold hundreds of thousands of pounds; the local bank into which the cash takings used to be banked had closed and once daily journeys to its further away located alternative had been reduced. "All you have to do is get us in," Lee continued, adding, "You can do that can't you? Normally I work alone, but sometimes a job takes two."

Over the next couple of weeks, they met again in the pub. Spike went systematically round the factory looking for weak spots that might afford entry. He reported back to Lee, who rejected most of them on some basis or another as unsuitable. Finally Spike suggested a men's room round the back of the works, in an office area only used by the design staff. He had found the window open a crack after the design team had gone home and there seemed to be no sign of it being linked to an alarm.

"Sounds like you've got it sorted," said Lee and then insisted that Spike come with him on the day, or rather the night. "Better with two," he told him, adding, "you can hold the torch and keep watch; it may be useful to have a second pair of hands."

Lee's manner seemed to brook no argument. Reluctantly Spike agreed. What had seemed a bit of an adventure at the start he now found somewhat scary, and so was Lee, his manner hardening as the due date got nearer. Frankly, he did not want to cross him.

On the night they each made their own way to the factory. Spike had left his bike there when he finished work, so he walked, from his terraced house a few blocks away, consciously seeking the darkest parts of the dark streets. The two men met in a small yard, under the chosen window, Lee was holding a canvas duffle bag. He held it up a little.

"For the cash," he said and grinned, a smile which seemed more menacing than friendly; it reminded Spike of a predatory animal.

Spike had left work at the factory a little late that day, after first ensuring the window was left open; it had been closed when he had gone to it, so he assumed someone thought everything was shut up.

"You go first," said Lee, checking that he was wearing gloves as instructed. "I'll give you a leg up then pass you the bag." It was a bit of a squeeze, but he got in, midst a good deal of shushing from Lee. He took the bag he was handed and called out: "Go to the side door, I'll unlock it for you." Once inside, Spike led the way through the dark deserted corridors to the small office where the safe was located. The whole place was eerily quiet. Their torches cast shifting shadows, which Spike found made Lee look nothing if not sinister.

"No problem, this model is like my party piece," said Lee looking at the safe.

"Here, hold my torch too, I need good light. Told you a job sometimes takes two."

Spike felt vulnerable and now really wished it didn't; but nevertheless, he resolved to get through the evening unscathed. He watched fascinated as Lee crouched in front of the safe, skilfully working on the tumblers and within ten minutes he heard the lock click open.

"Told you so. It's easy, easy money." He said and began to rake out bundles of bank notes from the bottom shelf as Spike knelt to put them into the bag. There seemed to be a great many, and he wondered what sum it added up to.

"How much do you think's here?" he asked, as he put in the last bundle. There was no reply and as he looked up, he saw Lee standing over him with an ugly black automatic pistol in his hand. The barrel was pointed straight at him. He froze.

"Thanks for your help," said Lee, "but you can identify me, and we can't have that now, can we? Besides the job might have needed two people, but there's more money for one."

Horrified Spike saw the line of Lee's mouth harden and his hand appear to tighten on the trigger. He struggled upright. Just then Lee's torch, balanced on the bag now full of cash that he clutched to his chest fell to the floor and went out. He was shaking. He realised that his own torch was now all that was providing illumination. Instinctively he switched it off, instantly enveloping the pair of them in total darkness as he simultaneously flung the bag straight at Lee and moved to one side. The gun went off with a sound that was ear splitting in the small office, but the bullet went wide. A pot plant on top of a filing cabinet behind him shattered and he heard the gun clatter to the floor. Lee was struggling to get to grips with the bag. Both his hands now free Spike dropped to the floor and found the gun. He stepped back. There was just a little light now that his eyes were getting used to the sudden darkness, and he saw the angry bulk of Lee as he threw himself across the room at him, a fierce roar leading the way.

Spike pushed his arms out to defend himself and, as Lee came close and pushed against him the gun which he now held became squashed between them and fired again, more muffled this time as the barrel was hard against Lee's anorak and chest. The big man slumped to the floor with a grunt and lay still. An acrid smell from the two shots hung in the air. The whole thing had taken only a few seconds.

Spike continued to shake, but in the silence that followed as he stood unmoving; he realised just how much things had turned his way. The money could all be his now. But his fear of being found out was becoming overpowering. What was he to do? Lee was a thug. He had been going to kill Spike. Now Lee was the dead one. Suddenly Spike could see a way out. He didn't have to take the money. He knew the company offered a reward as part of their overall security arrangements. That would do him. He had foiled a robbery: that would be his story, indeed a story he might sell to a newspaper, especially as he had survived a vicious attempt on his life too. He could get more money for that. He could be a hero; the death of Lee was surely just self-defence or no more than an accident. He'd tell them he had gone back for his bike, seen an open window and gone in to check it out. He reached for the phone on the desk and dialled 999.

"Police," he said when the operator asked which service he required. "I'm at..." He gave the address. "I think I've just foiled an armed robbery. But, but... the intruder's dead."

He was asked for his name and was told to remain there, but it was then agreed he would go to the front of the building to let the police inside. Suddenly, as he turned to leave the room, Lee moved a little and mumbled, "Help me." He clearly wasn't dead. Now what? Spike paused only for a second, then lent down, pressed the gun against Lee's chest, pulled the trigger and a second bullet completed the job, again leaving his ears ringing from the report.

As he straightened up, turned and left the room to meet the police at the main entrance, he muttered under his breath, "Like you kept on telling me, Lee, sometimes it takes two."

This story, "It takes two", has a crime theme and, as it turns out, two characters almost as bad as each other.

But not for lunch

The High Street was busy. He had driven round three times but had finally found a place to park. In recent years the town centre had become a nightmare, not only were there too few parking places, but the parking charges seemed to rise as one watched. This was, in the view of many people, killing the High Street, though this morning's experience had suggested the opposite; it was busy everywhere and busy in a slightly chaotic way. He was safely parked now, just where he wanted to be, but he had had to beat a woman to the space by an inch. He had sounded his horn and her nerve had cracked before his. She had glared at him, but he had left her no option but to drive on. He always hated trying to park in the High Street, it never seemed straightforward. Never mind, he told himself, he had an ideal place now; albeit on a yellow line, but he only planned a brief stop.

He wound down the window and lit a cigarette. He knew he should give up smoking, stop, but it calmed his nerves. As he brooded about this, he was startled by a loud rapping on the car roof just above his head. A woman stood alongside him, the woman he had beaten to the space he was now parked in.

"You should be ashamed of yourself, you stupid man." Her voice was an aggrieved shriek. "How dare you drive in such an aggressive manner, what have you got to say for yourself? You should know better." She rapped on the roof again with what he now saw was an umbrella.

"Clear off," he said, removing the cigarette from his mouth and expelling a cloud of smoke up towards the woman's face, making her take a step back. "Don't take it out on me just because you're a rotten driver."

"How dare you?" she began but the window closed in her face, and she saw the man at the wheel turn away.

This is all I need, thought James, willing the woman to go away and then noticing that while their exchange was going on a traffic warden had slapped a ticket on his windscreen. He had not seen him coming. He could see in the mirror that the angry woman was visible just behind the car, now in animated conversation with the warden. As he watched it became clear that the last thing the warden wanted was to get involved in their argument, he moved away and began to write another ticket a couple of cars further down the line. The woman glared at James's car again, took a step towards it, then, apparently thinking better of it, glared for a few seconds and turned away, heading for Marks & Spencer.

James heaved a sigh and took another drag on his cigarette. On reflection he felt ashamed and annoyed with himself. He should not have been so rude. It was a sign he thought that he was a little anxious. He had rather lost track of the time, but he realised that Joan would not be long now. As he thought this the back door of the car opened and Joan threw a large bag-for-life and a smaller Marks & Spencer bag onto the back seat.

"Okay, let's go," she said as she joined him in the front. James turned on the engine and drove out almost immediately, forcing an approaching car to brake and sound its horn at him as he did so. The traffic was busy but moving, and they quickly left the High Street behind and headed out of the town.

"Everything All right?" James enquired.

"Sure, no problem, can we go to Tesco next?"

James nodded and steeled himself for a tedious wait;

maybe, he thought, he could have a cup of coffee while Joan went round the aisles doing the shop. He parked up, easily this time, fumbled for a pound coin as he got out of the car then, wheeling a trolley, he led the way into the store. Joan allowed him to go for a coffee, promising to join him in the café before too long.

It was a couple of days later, on Thursday morning, that there was a knock on the door. It was the police, one in a regular suit and a uniformed constable.

"James Dixon?" The one in plain clothes holding out a badge identifying him as Inspector John Robinson voiced the question. A few minutes later James and his wife found themselves in sitting in their living room answering questions about a bank robbery.

"We know you were there," the Inspector told James. "You got a parking ticket."

"Yes, I fear I did," said James "but I went nowhere near the bank and Joan went to Marks & Spencer, she'll have the receipt, she always keeps her receipts, don't you dear?" Joan smiled and lent over to pick up her handbag.

The inspector soon discovered that was true; a receipt showed that Joan had been in M&S at the time. It was proving to be a fruitless line of enquiry, the Dixon's car had been parked close to the bank, the ticket and an angry woman called Sheila Jones confirmed that, but he saw that there was no evidence of any sort either of them had been the masked figure in the bank: the perpetrator had not spoken, simply passing a note across the counter and waving a pistol about in a gloved hand. There being no evidence and the old couple did appear to be rather unlikely bank robbers, after a few more questions the inspector excused himself and left, apologising as he did so.

"What a nice man," said Joan as they got ready to go

into town. James parked legally this time, though not without his well-rehearsed moan about the cost and held her hand and guided her towards their favourite coffee-shop in the High Street.

"The inspector was very polite, he seemed genuinely sorry to have inconvenienced us," Joan said as they entered the shop, then ordering tea and Victoria sponge and sitting in a corner booth.

"Everything's straight, isn't it? I changed the number plates on the car back to our own and I imagine you dealt with the gun, right?" Said James. The gun, a replica, had been hired.

"Yes, of course, young Eddie took it back in Tesco's. But I meant to ask, you said there was almost a hitch, what was that?" James reminded her about the race for the parking place, then told her about the angry woman and the parking ticket.

"The ticket didn't matter; indeed, I think it helped us with the police, but at the time I thought that woman was going to see you coming back to the car. But she'd gone by then, anyway, no harm done." In fact, the woman had not seen Joan, nor had anyone in the bank managed to get up from the prone position they had been required to adopt on the floor sufficiently quickly to see the couple drive away; besides, without the mask Joan would not look the least bit suspicious, just another retiree pottering about the town. The couple smiled at each other, and James sipped his tea.

"So, in fact it all went very well again, yes?" Said Joan. James nodded as he cut his cake.

"Yes, indeed, and I can't really believe that it's almost a year since I was retired early from the bank and sitting in our front room saying to you, 'What on Earth am I going to do with my time now I'm not going out to work?' You quoted that old saying at me, remember, about women marrying *for better or for worse, but not for lunch.* It would have been a crime just to sit around for hours watching daytime television, we'd have driven each other mad. But we've kept pretty busy since then, haven't we? We must think about what we do next. It will be your turn to drive."

Joan smiled at him and asked, "More tea? A nice cuppa always helps us think, then we have a bit of an errand to run before we go home." James nodded again and smiled at the thought as he turned to find a waitress.

Later, some thirty miles away the manager of local hospice shop had resolved to stop remonstrating with donors who ignored her notices and left bags outside in the doorway before the shop opened; she had changed her views when the last one left in such a way had turned out to contain more than £60,000 in bank notes.

I have followed tradition and given this book a title taken from one of one of the stories it contains. There is a pleasure in language that is short and yet encapsulates a significant amount, it is why many of us find an appeal in many a quotation, graffiti and more. In the writing world perhaps the best example of this is something said by Isaac Asimov (a prolific writer, he wrote more than four hundred books, and is perhaps best known for his science fiction). Once asked what he would do if told he had only six months to live, he thought for a moment and replied in just two words: "Type faster." That not only brings a smile but says so much about his attitudes to his work as a writer. Wonderful. That said, I love the saying, said of marriage at the time of retirement, "You marry them for better or for worse, but not for lunch"; an easy choice for this book's title.

None like it hot

God, it's hot. Outside the hot wind is whipping dust into the air; this and the inherent heat haze reduce the visibility. I know I'm lucky to live on a hill, I have a view out to sea and get something of a breeze and that helps a little. Years ago, before global warming took its toll and sea levels rose, much of the sea I now count as a wonderful view on a clear day would have been land, a stretch of the Suffolk countryside that ran inland from the East coast. The land around me is now parched, dusty and any vegetation is sparse.

I want to record something else though. Remember that it was technology that saved us. Well, the pace at which the world changed its ways was too slow to halt global warming, as were politicians, but technological development eventually made it possible to live with the results, or at least for a much-reduced population to do so. Here in the U.K. the latter part of the 21st century was not pretty, there were riots and food shortages, and of course rising sea levels meant that massive tracts of land disappeared leaving people owning coastal property dispossessed; the scale was way beyond comprehension. The government had enough problems; individual householders whose precious home had been washed away were far down the queue and left to their own devices. Around the world millions died quickly, with places like Bangladesh wiped out as the sea rose way beyond what could be contained.

Now, as I say, technology has helped us to live in the new climate. Artificial intelligence had become sufficiently advanced just in time. The A.I.s see to everything, maintaining power, producing food and water, monitoring, indeed initiating, communications. Without air conditioning this house would be well-nigh uninhabitable. And it's the technology that I want to write about.

Pause computer. I need a drink.

Okay write on again. Computer: record this.

Where was I? Oh yes, the problem with the technology.

The trouble is that the technology is now faltering, certainly much of it is, perhaps all of it. When I woke this morning the air conditioning was off. To say it was hot hardly covers it. The diagnostics gave no reason for it, why it went off is a mystery, as is why it came back on again an hour later. Last time I drove out to get supplies the car suddenly veered off the road. No warning. Luckily there was no other traffic and it lost power as well, so it just ran onto the verge and stopped. Diagnostics were off then too. It only lasted a few minutes. I was still sitting in the car wondering what to do when the power came on again. It drove me home okay, but I guess it could happen again. It seems likely and I fear it will.

I've reported such incidents, of course I have, and the news feed is reporting a range of similar occurrences all over the country, a growing number of such occurrences in fact and without a hint being given as to what might be the cause. Some of these failures are serious: evidently a whole food factory has done nothing for several weeks and has virtually been written off, several large areas have been flooded as pumps working to keep out the sea have failed, lives have been lost. Cars seem to be developing minds of their own and, though once infallible, they are now involved in a growing number of accidents.

Of course, the government assure us that they are investigating; every A.I in the country is being turned towards the search for a cause... and a cure. Rumours are rife: is it an endemic fault, something inadvertently built into the computers years ago that is only now showing itself? Is it some sort of overload, are the systems simply being stretched beyond their capacity to work efficiently? There are even some people who put it down to sabotage. After all there are countries very much worse off than we are here, places from which people would quickly come in and take us over if they could drive us out. That's not a pleasant thought. The population here is now tiny. The automatic defences at our boundaries are all that is keeping us from being taken over by refugees; the thought of that technology failing is not a good one. And recent summers seems to have got hotter and hotter. With no rain for more weeks than I can count, most of our drinking water must now be coming from the desalination plants on the coast and if such facilities fail, well, the result does not bear thinking about.

The government initially kept this growing technological breakdown secret. But the rumours became so overpowering that in the last few weeks it had to admit the scale of the problem, it had to allow the A.I.s to report the news. The cause is not only still not known, and the problems getting worse, but it also seems that it is worldwide, and worse already in many places than it is here. An international effort is evidently now underway to sort things out, but some places have gone silent, whole countries are silent, and the A.I.s actually conducting the investigation and looking for the reason for failure and a solution are themselves clearly working less and less well.

Computer, computer, nothing I say is being recorded.

Damn and blast. Computer! That's another system down.

I managed to print out my recent diary pages, but I am having to write new entries by hand now. Things are much worse. Any news is intermittent now and none of it is good. I have been rationing myself, but my supplies have finally run out. The car stopped working weeks ago, and though I try it every day it shows no sign of returning to a working condition and charging it makes no difference. It is too far to walk to the nearest supply point, though I reckon I might be able to get some food from the sea, which is now only about three hundred yards away. It will be a struggle in this heat, but I must try, what else can I do? I must do it alone too, I have no near neighbours, the nearest stopped answering my calls months ago, and the phone network has been dead now for ages.

If I could leave walking to a supply point until the weather changes, until the summer heat drops just a little, it might be easier, but I can't wait, I simply must go now. Maybe I'll find a bicycle on the way, that would help. Anyway, winter is hot too, so waiting might not help very much and the changes to the weather continue: in recent months the temperature has hit record highs yet again and when it does rain the storms are vicious. Indeed, it occurs to me as I set off that this current period may not just be the hottest on record, there is every chance of it being my last summer on Earth.

I am afraid I am somewhat pessimistic about global warming. Scientists have been sounding warnings for decades and if anything, we regularly find their predictions have underestimated the severity of the likely impact. Politicians meanwhile are fixated on the short term, largely fail to understand the problem – one which surely needs massive international collaboration, something else they are not good at – and it is clear, to quote actress Lily Tomlin that: "Things are going to get worse, before they get worse." So, the inspiration for this story is not difficult to see. On a lighter note, I like a title that is a play on words, or which twists a well-known phrase (or in this case a film title), hence "None like it hot".

Something of an obsession

"What do you think, John?" I looked up to see the questioner focussed exclusively on me and others sitting around me at the table watching. I should have been paying more attention, but I had been miles away. I had been distracted, I knew that, but I couldn't stop thinking about her. To be honest I had found myself besotted with her and the feeling had intensified over what was now a matter of maybe almost three months.

She wasn't classically beautiful, but she had caught my eye as I commuted and since then I had seen her regularly on the train that we both take to work. The train is always busy, and I don't know where she starts her journey, certainly far enough before me for her always to get a seat. By the time I have scanned the few carriages she seems to favour near the centre of the train from the platform to see exactly where she is, I never get a seat. So, I must stand, clinging on to one of the upright rails for thirty minutes, uncaring about the discomfort and trying not to be seen to be staring, though I have caught her eye more than once.

There is something about her. I have no idea what she does, in fact, I don't really know anything about her, how could I? Nevertheless, I was just somehow certain she would be nice to know; from the first day she caught my eye I knew, I knew at once. One morning she was reading a book, well actually she always seems to read a book – I like that too, I love reading – but this one was clearly amusing and for a few days she smiled regularly to herself as she read. She had a lovely smile; it made her face light up and once or twice her smile widened still more at something in the book, and I was entranced at the sight. I reckon she was a little embarrassed to be seen smiling in public, more so when she laughed out loud at one point. She paused in her reading and brushed her hair aside in a gesture I had seen her use often. It was pretty hair too, brown, slightly curly and with an attractive hint of the untameable about it. Other things too seemed to suggest a glimpse into her character.

For instance, whenever the train is running late – and sadly these days that is a regular occurrence – you can at once feel the change in the demeanour of most of the passengers aboard. People become tense, they become restless, those sitting next to someone they know exchange comments about it, muttering about, "Bloody rail workers" and complaining of what a late arrival will mean to them – "I can't be late again, my boss will kill me." She, I didn't know her name then, of course, never seemed to get upset. She would sometimes pause in her reading and look at her watch but would then quickly turn back to the page; buried in an enjoyable book she probably finds the time goes by quickly. If the lateness bothered her, she didn't let it show. I like that too.

I always watch as she gets off the train, having positioned myself so that she is nearer the door than me. She's about five foot five, I think, about my own age and she has a nice figure and a jaunty step. Can you step off a train with a jaunty step? Well, she does. Putting her book in the satchel-style bag she always carries she gets up and heads off, presumably to where she works, and I stand there thinking for the umpteenth time of ways of starting a conversation with her. I pray that one day she will leave her book on the seat and that I can catch her up and return it, making a winning comment as I do so. But she never fails to store it carefully away in her bag. I have considered following her to see where she goes, but that would make me late for work and I have never done so, besides, it could easily come over as creepy. Well, maybe one day. I must do something. One day I have told myself, one day I will do something, something that will bring us together. I am not letting it go.

Then the man's voice from the other end of the table brings me back to the moment and interrupts my thoughts.

"John – are you on strike or something. Come on you must have some opinion."

I had still been miles away. I had already realised that my fantasies were interfering with my life, my work, with everything I tried to do; that is especially so today. Of course, it is. I didn't seem able to maintain my concentration for even two minutes at a time. I knew I had to do something about the situation, and had resolved to do just that, after all I had been pondering about it for weeks. I drew myself back to the moment.

It had been a bit of a shock to see my "railway girl" somewhere other than on the train when I sat down in my allotted seat and saw her across the room. I knew her name now, Jolie Brown, and a good deal more about her and how she conducted herself too. She had a lovely voice, firm but melodious, and during the proceedings she had occasionally flicked her hair back in that oh so familiar gesture I had come to love. For all my daydreaming I reckoned I had followed matters closely: finally, now I forced myself to concentrate on the question I'd been asked. Though I had no intention of letting go of the image of her face, for the moment at least I tried hard to push it to the back of my mind as I turned towards my questioner. I knew my obsession had become awkward – inappropriate is a much better word in the current circumstances – and given the position

Jolie was in. I looked round the circle of faces of those sitting at the table before I replied.

"Right," I said, "let me tell you what I think." I had everyone's attention and continued speaking with my eyes locked on the foreman of the jury.

Sometimes having an enigmatic ending to a short story seems to be the right thing, and that was certainly the case here with "Something of an obsession", in which the outcome for both the key protagonists is left untold and various possibilities about what may happen next remain open. You must decide.

A meeting will sort it out

"Well, good morning, everyone, I've called this meeting for very specific reasons so let's get down to business straight away, shall we?"

First, let me say that I'm sorry the meeting had to be called at such short notice. But it is urgent, and it is important. I am sorry too that there was confusion about where it was to be held. The conference room was already booked, well actually it's being redecorated, and I can't abide the smell of paint. So, I was forced to make alternative arrangements; thank you Paul for squeezing us all into your office even though it is rather small. I hope you are okay sat on that stool, Paul. The result of all this is that the meeting is starting nearly half an hour late. Despite that, I know Barry's not here yet, but he will just have to catch up when he arrives; something about a school visit he said – some people have no sense of priorities and that seems to apply to Barry more than most; that man's always ducking and diving – now I think of it, there are two things I dislike about that man – his face. But let's move on – the coffee is due to arrive soon.

The team convened here is very important: you all know Mary is our financial guru and so obviously no new plans can be made without involving her – more's the pity, her motto seems to be that everything needs complications and delay adding to it. Not that there seems to be money for anything at present. These may be hard times, but money is for investing in the business, Mary. Your role is not to protect it like a broody mother hen sitting on her eggs – you must break open the corporate piggy bank occasionally and actually *spend* a little. Well, a lot in the case of this project. Mind you that was a good cost-cutting idea that you emailed me about yesterday, we must check what the men in the group think about it.

John is here because he will, in his usual fumbling way, attempt to project manage any new scheme and Jane, as our Human Resources expert, will no doubt tell us that Health and Safety and Employment Law procedures mean we can't do anything when we want, how we want or in some cases at all, without risking the wrath of the law, jumping us into a time consuming and expensive employment tribunal or bringing everyone out on strike. You will all remember the fiasco of firing that idiot in research. He disobeyed direct orders. He was shoddy, constantly late and wasted precious research money. And he burnt down the research lab for goodness sake – you can still smell smoke in many parts of the building – but it still took ten months to fire him by the time we had issued all the necessary warnings, initiated the labyrinthine disciplinary procedures and dotted all the i's and crossed all the t's. He was able to stay on long enough to almost gas his assistant – poor Julie was in hospital for a week, I think – and get us blacklisted by the Research Council. It was a total bloody disaster and all too typical of how things seem to work around here nowadays.

Anyway, the rest of you know your roles and Paul, well I sometimes think you are at every meeting that takes place in the building, indeed I sometimes think you do little else *but* attend meetings, and here you are again, though I'm not sure what you can contribute. And no Paul – don't speak yet – when I want your opinion, I'll give it to you.

Right, moving swiftly on. This is potentially a very important project. Moreover, it seems to me to be the only way forward and I cannot recommend it highly enough. There may be other ways of proceeding, and my setting out a plan that we do things this way is, of course, only a suggestion; though that said I hope you will bear in mind who's making it. I very much want inputs from everyone, I want any decision to be a consensus and I want to hear what you have to say and to suggest. No, not yet, Paul, as I've said when I want your opinion, I'll give it to you.

The trouble is too many people around the organisation are downright unproductive. For instance, half the customer service team seem to spend all their time surfing the internet rather than talking to customers, and tweeting or "facebooking" or whatever it is. Or worse: I read somewhere that 70% of all the hits on pornography sites are made between the hours of 9 and 5, no wonder customers are complaining. We must get people to pull their socks up, gird up their loins and get down to some real work. Times are hard, the market is fickle and don't get me started on the way government intervention makes things worse. I know it's difficult to see the writing on the wall when your back's to it, but we have to re-double our efforts and get things really buzzing. I mustn't be condescending, but there's no excuse for procrastination. You *do* all know what that means *don't you*? Quiet Paul, I'm sure you do, especially as you're so very good at it.

Oh, *do* come in Barry, here you are at last. No, don't apologise, we knew you were going to be late and had more important things to do than join this meeting on time. Help yourself to some coffee; no, don't actually – it's not arrived yet.

Right, we must wrap it up now. I for one have a more

important meeting to get to. We've covered a lot of ground this morning, I think it has been very useful, but clearly no decision can be made today. Think about it and we will meet again soon. Trust me: we will get this right if we all pull together. Thank you all for your contributions today. No Paul, say no more now for goodness sake, save it for the next meeting... besides, and I'm sure I've said this already, when I want your opinion, I'll give it to you.

And just one more thing I should perhaps have mentioned earlier: Mary perhaps you would write up the minutes for this meeting. And this time try and get them round to everyone *before* we meet again, will you. Oh, here's the coffee – about time too – but wasted, such a pity we must all get on. And one more final thing – next time we meet let's have a bit more order, shall we? It's very distracting if you all talk while I'm interrupting."

Occasionally a monologue is the best form to adopt. I seem to have spent a great deal of time in meetings over the years and it has to be said a proportion of them were annoying, decided little or nothing or, at worst, were a complete waste of time. "A meeting will sort it out" may be exaggerated but I believe it reflects some truths too. For the record, meetings need a clear purpose, a clear agenda and with good communication, including chairmanship, can find solutions, spark ideas and see decisions made that create real opportunities. <u>Note:</u> one of my business books is "Meetings: an agenda for success" (published by Legend Press).

Marking time

I have always been good with gadgets. I was writing programs for my computer in primary school, and I built my own desktop then too, making many of the parts from scratch. If I'm going to tell you this with any hope of you believing me, let me emphasise – I have always been good with gadgets.

That early experience is what got me into designing chips and that in turn got me into more advanced areas too. Though I say so myself I am surprisingly good at this sort of stuff. I was making good money selling my work to Microsoft in my teens, but now this new situation is beyond it all. It's, well, it's epic. Truly. I have built my own time machine. Right, I know, I know. You don't believe me. But it's true and it works. And it's small enough to wear on my wrist. Of course, it is only a prototype, it still needs some fine tuning. Now, don't look like that, it really is true.

But I've got a problem. I should never have shown it off in public. I couldn't resist it. I got talking to a few friends, and once I'd mentioned its existence, they demanded a demonstration. Just a little one I thought, where is the harm in that? I set things up, told them to check on me in an hour and disappeared into the future. It's instant. No flashing lights, no fading away, no smoke or sparks; from their perspective I was just... well, gone. I don't know what they did for an hour, but when they caught up and I appeared again, they were all sitting around looking at their watches and when I popped up exactly on cue, wow, you should have seen their faces. For me the process was instantaneous, of course, I hopped straight forward an hour and there they all were, sitting looking puzzled.

This happened before I discovered one small snag. I did say it was a prototype, I said it needed work, and above all I told my friends not to mention its existence. But of course, my demonstration was all over social media within hours and now some dubious bunch of ruthless, lowlife crooks are after it and they are quite prepared to kill me for it too; I realise that the thing must be worth an absolute fortune. So here I am. Having been grabbed in the street, bundled into a car and driven who knows where for an hour or so with a hood over my head, I find myself in an anonymous room sitting at a table. It might be a routine board meeting but for the gun, the knives and the looks the other five people present are giving me.

"Hand it over," says the one who appears to be in charge. He sounds like he might be negotiating for something as routine as a building contract, or some-such, he's very matter of fact, but he looks as if he lost his last scruple a very long time ago. He nods to his colleague with the gun. The man's huge, he looks like he could crush me with a single blow, nevertheless he settles for lining the pistol he is holding in one huge fist up on my chest; it's steady as a rock. I bluster.

"I can't just take it off, it's sensitive, it needs resetting now, I must..." I want to suggest that it's time locked like a safe, but he interrupts:

"Just take it off or my friend here will take it off for you – with your hand as well if necessary." The leader speaks impassively, but I have no trouble believing him. Another of the group, presumably the aforementioned friend, stabs a knife into the table to reinforce his point.

"Put some music on," says the leader, "it will drown

out his screams, we don't want the neighbours kicking up, now do we." Somewhere behind me Billie Holiday starts singing "Pennies from Heaven". I'm a jazz fan so bizarrely the thought occurs to me that this is rather nice. He may be going to have me maimed, but the man has good taste; ridiculous thought, and I'm set to get more than rain showers to spoil my day. The volume is turned right up to a level where the pitch makes something in the corner of the room start buzzing discordantly as the sound vibrates around the room. The buzzing sets my teeth on edge even before the giant stands up and begins to walk round the table towards me; the knife he is holding glints in the light.

Quickly I reach my right hand across and tap the face of the gadget, which is on my left wrist.

"Wait, wait. It will take a moment," I say, still playing for time and trying to think fast.

In fact, what I did took only a split second. I pressed the main button and disappeared. Suddenly they saw the room as empty. In the same chair having moved an hour on I too found the room was empty. They had gone, presumably mystified, but also doubtless convinced the device worked. I crept out of the room and managed to leave the house unseen. Outside what proved to be a row of terraced houses, I found I was still in London, a street sign mentioned Stoke Newington. They must have driven me round in circles to disguise where we were taking me. Sooner after I had reached my apartment, a journey involving half an hour on a bus, than I was grabbed again; in the same place and in the same way. Which brings me to the snag.

Currently my device will only take me one single hour forward or back. No further. Exactly an hour, not even a minute more. I know I can work on it and make it better. The principle's established, the quantum flux is... sorry let's ignore the principle, you wouldn't understand it. But currently it means there's no time for the work needed. I may escape them, but I can't go far enough away to give me time to research it, refine it and extend the time over which it works. Nor can I reappear somewhere else. The gadget will only move me through time, not through space. So, in fact if only they knew, all they have to do when I vanish is wait. Then I'd be finished, I'd reappear right in front of them exactly an hour later.

It's a bleak situation and the worst thing is that now it's happened three times – being caught and vanishing that is – and what's happening seems to be creating some sort of weird quantum loop in time. Even I don't understand how or why that is, least of all how to stop it. Because the setting is always for an hour, because I can't change things and because the proton alignment field is increasingly out of flux with – sorry, don't worry about that – it just means the loop becomes repetitive. It locks in and it seems that it can't be changed. I'm not dead yet and I still have the device strapped firmly to my wrist, but I can't see any way out. If anything, the loop seems to be getting worse.

There must be a way, there must. I made the wretched thing; I must be able to improve it. All I need first is some time: a decent jump – a month ahead say, a week even might do it. Then I could fix it. I would have enough time to work on it, and I could then lose them forever. It must be possible. Surely, I can do it. I know I can do it. I just have to get out of this damn loop.

So, the question now is: what do I do next?

I have always been good with gadgets. I was writing programs for my computer in primary school, and I built my own laptop then too...

Oh, damn and blast!

The genre of "Marking time" is science fiction I suppose,

and writing anything about such a much-visited idea as time travel demands finding something which is a little bit different from what others have done in the past. I hope this achieves that, now... I have always been good with gadgets. I was writing programs for my computer in primary school, and I built my own laptop... sorry, just kidding!

Seasonal Health and Safety

Fred had been unlucky. His job involved all sorts of things and generally speaking he enjoyed it all and felt he was good at it too. But it demanded some flexibility. That was usually okay also but, just occasionally, a job arrived that was, well, more difficult and certainly less likely to please. His colleague Joe called such things Black Hole jobs and defined them as the kind of thing that ate up time, where the nature of it made it impossible to get things completely right, and, perhaps worst of all, where you were bound to end up upsetting someone.

"You've drawn the short straw this time and no mistake, old chap." Joe had said to him when the memo had arrived, "no one has ever organised the department's Christmas party without hitting some problems. I don't envy you. You've not done it before, have you?"

"Well, no, what about you?" Replied Fred, already beginning to feel he had been right to see the task as undesirable.

"Oh, yes, albeit many years ago, but I still feel the pain. I dressed up as Father Christmas, I even got some reindeer in, but that was a mistake. They ate all the mince pies and after an hour we had sh... that is droppings all over the floor. The boss was furious. Never again. I wish you luck."

His comments hardly filled Fred with confidence. When the memo had arrived, he had initially felt it would be a good thing to do, after all it was the festive season, and the party was just for those working in the admin department. Now he had very much changed his mind. The more he thought about it the more difficult the task seemed to look. Food, decorations and so much more – what about Father Christmas? Should he dress up as Joe had done? He resolved at once to very definitely omit any hint of reindeer. He wanted no part of anything that needed a shovel. Then another complication came to mind. He turned back to Joe who, sitting nearby at the desk, was completing the registration details for a new arrival. The new arrival, a kindly looking old man with white hair and huge steel rimmed glasses, stood in front of him. Fred didn't interrupt them.

"I'd never have thought one's first experience of Heaven would be form filling," the man said.

"Nearly done," replied Joe. "Things must be done right you know, though I must admit it is all a somewhat bureaucratic process. Now if you just let me have your glasses, we'll be done." The man looked worried.

"But I can't see without…" Joe interrupted him.

"No need here, your eyesight is perfect, give it a go, the glasses can go back down below to Oxfam." As the man handed them over and headed off towards the door marked "Border Crossing", a sign he found he could read perfectly easily, he muttered to himself. "Well, I never."

That exchange finished, Fred quizzed Joe further.

"One thing," he said, "do we have to keep operations running during the party?"

"Of course we do," replied Joe, "someone's bound to die during the proceedings, there's a great big world down there you know." Fred looked out of the window across the seemingly endless banks of clouds and replied simply, "I suppose so," though he thought too of the occasional failings in the system; only that morning another fanatic had turned up demanding an unlimited number of virgins and had had to be rerouted. He wasn't pleased. Yes, a duty roster was just one of the many things he would have to arrange.

It was, as Joe had predicted, a difficult task. The admin department in Heaven also saw to all admissions and was known as ARS: short for Admin & Registration Section, a name Fred had always seen as a little unfortunate. The list of angels assigned to staff it consisted of 42 individuals. This was a number chosen not just so as to comfortably handle the department's various tasks, after all everything here was comfortable, it wouldn't be Heaven otherwise, but also because Douglas Adams had decided that 42 was the answer to the question of life, the universe and everything, and Gabriel, who was their immediate boss, thought that a great joke seeing as how little people on Earth actually knew about anything. So, Fred had to cater for that number, judge the quantity of turkey, mince pies and so on to keep everyone happy, and judge also the right amount of wine and other drinks to go with it all. It meant quite a bit of organisation and gaining the collaboration of a number of other people.

First, he divided the party attendees into seven groups; then he drew straws as to who would be on duty for which part of the proceedings so that no one missed too much of the party. Then he had to call in a few favours from several back-up departments to help staff to prepare and serve the food. It had to be admitted that despite all the joys of being an angel, the wings could cause problems, and moving round a crowded room with a tray of sausage rolls or whatever without knocking over those behind you as you turned did not make that a popular assignment. Nevertheless, Fred was good at his job – he even persuaded a group of new arrivals, all killed together at another party when a faulty gas fitting exploded, to decorate the Christmas tree. Doing so only cheered them up a little and Fred wondered, not for the first time, why such disasters were allowed to happen; the answer to that was, he decided, simply above his pay grade, however, he knew they would settle in before long.

Music was another problem. What to choose. Fred was a jazz fan, but some of his colleagues had been "upstairs" as it were for a very long time and saw anything not played on a lyre as sacrilege. More recent arrivals were fixated on The Beatles, or something called Take That, the latter a sound which had mercifully passed Fred by. He rejected choirs, however heavenly, as likely to overpower the occasion, and decided on a medley that changed style pretty regularly and which he hoped would keep everyone happy. Then he found a teenager, well someone who had died as a teenager, who understood the technology, to record it onto some gadget that would play it on the day. He saw to the decorations himself, putting up multi-coloured lights, streamers and getting a junior colleague to nip "downstairs" to pick up a real tree and some mistletoe and holly. He even sprinkled some artificial snow around. He could easily have got some real snow, there were plenty of clouds around after all, but he decided that would quickly melt and create a slipping hazard. He was conscious that, before the event could go ahead, the whole set up would have to undergo an inspection by Gabriel, who was the ultimate boss on such matters, and he would doubtless arrive with an underling ready to do a health and safety assessment. What nonsense thought Fred, after all we are all guaranteed good health here. He supposed it was just that some habits were difficult to break; anyway, it was true to say that Gabriel had always been a bit of a jobsworth all said and done.

On the morning of the party Gabriel duly arrived and toured the party room. Fred was pleased with his reaction. His sidekick made notes on a clipboard that Fred hoped were mostly ticks. It took a while, then came his judgement:

"Well done, Fred, you appear to have done a very good job," he was told seriously. "But..." Gabriel continued and Fred was not really surprised, thinking that the initial reaction had perhaps all been too good to be true, though he could not think what Gabriel had found wanting and needing a "but".

"What is it, is something wrong?" Asked Fred, still searching for something amidst his many arrangements that he felt could be described as inappropriate.

"You really need to ask?" Said Gabriel, but before he could continue, he was interrupted by an arrival at the check in desk just behind them, the noise from which seemed to indicate a problem. He turned away from Fred.

"Excuse me a moment," he said over his shoulder, "we appear to have a problem with a new arrival." He turned towards a tall, distinguished looking man wearing a pin-striped suit.

"Oh, hello Minister," he went on, "whatever are you doing here? No, no, no - given your recent behaviour in the House of Commons I fear you need to retrace your steps and turn the other way." Gabriel left arranging this redirection to the angel on duty at the desk and turned back to resume his conversation with Fred.

"You see Fred," he continued in a patient tone, "as the Minister there demonstrates so clearly, there have been more than enough problems with hands on knees lately - now whatever do you think would happen if I allowed you to keep the mistletoe up?"

There is often room for a Christmas story in the festive season and "Seasonal Health and Safety" is one of two stories here written to fit that role. The second in this collection follows. I hope both raise a smile. The ending of this one strikes a topical note that was, in part, what prompted the story.

Ding dong grumpily on high

The morning is cold. I see flakes of snow wafting in the air and blurring the view a little as I look out of the window. Given what day it is there are just enough snowflakes falling to make you think of sleigh bells and mistletoe and get traffic, in the UK at least, gearing up to turn into solid gridlock once the number of flakes settling has reached double figures. Somewhere, a room or two away, someone clicks on a radio.

Oh... no, no, no, it's that damn tune again. I sometimes think that if I hear the infuriating refrain of, *We wish you a merry Christmas* one more time I'll smash the radio to bits. And it's not just the radio either, such music starts playing everywhere – in shops, pubs and lifts – and does so what seems like it is an absolute age before the Christmas season. Of course, I could never actually say, "Bah, humbug", about Christmas, I love it really. But it's always the same as the festive season approaches, something it seems to do faster and faster too these days, one minute it's Easter Eggs, then summer holidays and then, before you know it, it's all, "Ho, Ho, Ho", there's holly impaling you all over the house and the time necessary to do the many things that need to be done before the big day need squeezing into a shorter and shorter period of time. There's just so much to arrange and not only to arrange but also to agree with others; after all Christmas is a family time.

For instance, where will this year's Christmas dinner

take place? Last year ours was at my sister's house. Easy enough you say: just turn up and eat. Not so, not so at all, oh dear me no. Weeks, no months, beforehand the whole family was conferring about every tiny detail – who would buy the turkey (it had to be a turkey of course, very traditional, my sister), who would pay for it, how big it should be, whether it should be a fresh one – though actually everyone agreed about that – certainly my sister wants it so fresh she is putting it into the oven only a split second after the last feather is removed. And all those decisions are tied in with various members of the family making up their minds about whether they plan to be present or not. And then there's what should go with the turkey? How many of those likely to be present like stuffing? What about sausages? Some of us hate Brussel sprouts, but again they are traditional, so a perfect mix of vegetables must be worked out. Then there are all the other trimmings and arrangements: everything from crackers, to be judged by the volume of the bang and the cringe-making nature of the jokes they contain, and such things as nuts and dates, right through to who sits next to who. If Uncle Arthur is anywhere near Aunt Maud again then we will be in for another lengthy tirade from her about how he repeatedly pulled her pigtails when she was eight. It may have scarred her for life but reliving it endlessly in front of the whole family is certainly not the epitome of festive cheer for everyone else. It's proved better over the years to get her to concentrate on giving a comprehensive review of the Christmas tree decorations, even though they are usually judged to be never "half as good as last year", and whoever got the short straw to arrange them is usually totally entangled in the wiring for the lights and in tears after the first fifteen minutes.

Preparation is a long, wearisome business and other things don't stop just because Christmas is coming;

some of us have lives, some of us have other responsibilities and I for one have a living to earn too, for goodness sake. Perhaps we should just book a restaurant for lunch and have done with it, but have you seen what that costs these days? Given the current cost of posting cards, you would need to start saving for it even earlier than my sister starts asking Christmas questions. Maybe I should *open* a restaurant, not only might I make some money but what I had to do for Christmas lunch would then be fixed and firm: okay, busy too, but fixed and firm.

And the whole blessed process all takes such a long, long time. The first Christmas card catalogue usually drops on the doormat during August. The shop windows acquire a Christmassy look soon after, just as the music turns Christmassy and of late the so-called January sales seem to start in November; we may hope Christmas will be white, but these days some of the store sales are black; and on a Friday.

Preparations are stretched over months and months. I never start it. The reason the family so often gathers at my sister's is that she begins her, "What-about-arrangements-for-Christmas-this-year-it-will-be-here-before-you-know-it" questioning so very early; we all just say, "Why don't you do it?" to ensure that we get things settled and because we know she wants that really. Even while Boxing Day is still fresh in the mind and long before New Year is upon us the questions start. Damn it, last year most of Boxing Day itself was taken up with discussions about the coming year; we were not allowed to sit down to lunch until we had gathered round the computer and prepared a full-blown spreadsheet for goodness sake. And some of us even missed watching the monarch on Christmas afternoon as the task of making "who will do what when next year" lists was continued for a while before we even left the lunch table.

Now, before you know it, the whole business is upon us again. Indeed, there is now little more than 24 hours to go. What's not agreed and fixed by now is not going to get fixed at all, much less agreed. However, I'm sure everything will be All right – besides it's really for the children and they will love it almost whatever we do. So, enough of this blather; of course it's a problem to get everything organised, of course we all wish it were simpler, of course there is the odd thing that gets forgotten, but I can't go on fussing about it forever and it really is a wonderful time of the year, I can't wait for a nice turkey lunch and as it's at my sister's house again I am sure it will all be just wonderful.

There are still a few more things for me to do. Not the beer, I got that in and a really good brew too, not just what was on special offer in the supermarket; it is Christmas after all, and I don't want some old rubbish that tastes better coming up than going down. What else? Well, most important of all, I must set Doctor Who to record. It's a must for me, though my sister hates it; she says it's silly and just too far-fetched, so that's one for me to watch later. Mind you she has her favourite programmes and will certainly factor watching the Christmas edition of Call the Midwife into her timetable; no problem there though, I like that too.

But time marches on – now what else must I do? Hang on, another interruption, that's the front doorbell. It will be carol singers, I just know it will; they turn up every Christmas Eve at about this time without fail – the tuneless performing for the uninterested again, I'll bet. I want to shout, "Go away, we're all too busy", but I won't. I don't want to seem grumpy and cantankerous, well not too much so anyway.

"Answer the door someone, and feel free to give them a mince pie or two but do mention that they're only just out of the freezer, broken teeth won't improve their tempers, or their singing either for that matter. Try to smile at them, and then turn the radio up so we won't really hear what they sing. Luckily other things about Christmas are guaranteed to delight – I can't wait till tomorrow and I'm sure all the arrangements will all be fine. Now, excuse me, but some of us really *must* get on. I've things to do, places to go as they say... See you later everyone – I must get my chores done on time. Come on, Rudolf, let's go deliver."

Another Christmas tale written for and read at a Christmas party of my local u3a group (University of the Third Age), and which raised a few smiles.

No blame

"Don't worry, Ian, it was not meant to be, and you did your best". The man was dressed in green hospital scrubs and hurried out before Ian could even see who he was. But he knew one thing; if anyone else told him it was "All right" he might well hit them. He lent forward in his chair, elbows on knees and pushed his head into his hands.

It had not been a good day. The usual minor annoyances had come in spades: his alarm clock failed to go off, and he had woken late drenched in sweat and with a dream of some ill-defined horror fading rapidly. In his rush to catch up on time he had cut himself shaving, and the plaster on his chin still bore testament to his hurry. He was a surgeon for god's sake, how could he cut himself shaving? Then his car had failed to start, and he had waited for what seemed like hours until the taxi he called arrived, then paid for time spent sitting in the biggest traffic jam in living memory. When he at last reached the hospital, he was distinctly late, and a full operating list awaited. His mood had not affected his work though, once scrubbed up and in the operating theatre he was his usual professional self, and even managed not to growl at his team.

As he brooded on the day past, the door to the changing area opened and another voice began, "I heard what happened, don't blame yourself." He didn't, but he did want a bit of peace and quiet. He waved the sympathetic colleague away and slammed out.

He walked to the far end of the corridor and lay down on the narrow bed in the cramped cubbyhole used by doctors on night call. He thought back to one of the morning's operations. The patient had been brought in from a traffic accident, he had been the victim of a hit and run driver. He was only young, in his early twenties; as yet no one even knew his name. With multiple injuries, and heavily drugged to stop the pain, he had never spoken a word. Once he had opened him up the severity of the injuries was all too plain to see. He had tried various procedures, but he knew from the first moment that it was hopeless. He was unable to stem the multiple bleeds, no one could have done anything, and the patient had died on the operating table. He knew it was not his fault, sadly these things happened; most days the balance was good, and he saved lives, but you never got used to the times when it ended in failure. It did matter, and it was almost impossible not to become involved. He muttered, "Sorry" under his breath and then he must have dozed off, because the next thing he was aware of was a loud ringing. He snapped awake and swung his feet off the narrow bed. Smoke was curling under the door. "A fire, bloody obviously," he thought as he wondered what to do. He had no idea where the fire was, how bad it was or how long it had been underway. But he was in a windowless room barely ten-foot square and with a single door that was the only way out. He felt his heart beating faster and he found time to wonder if his recent dream had been about a fire. He had no option but to open the door.

The corridor was smoky, but he could see along it, certainly he saw the green emergency exit light shining above the door at the end of the corridor where both the lift and stairs were situated. He went back into the room, grabbed a towel and sloshed water onto it from the little basin in the corner. Holding it over his face he went out and hurried down the corridor. He saw no one; he must have slept through the evacuation. Halfway along the corridor he saw flames as he passed a glass fronted door, immediately after he passed there was an explosion in the room, he turned to see the door blown out and a swirl of flame billowing into the corridor. He speeded up; so did his heart rate. There must have been oxygen tanks in the room he thought and if he was right then there might be more to come.

As he reached the end of the corridor, he heard another explosion and this time he felt the heat singe his back. He was on the tenth floor, so it would take a while to get out. As he pulled the door to the stair well open, the lift door right alongside it opened. The smoke had thickened, and the lift already had smoke in it, but he could just see that the light was on and the figure of a man inside. Vaguely remembering fire drills from the past, he muttered, "Never go in the lift", but as he did so two further explosions behind him punched out a blast of hot air and pitched him forward onto the floor. The man in the lift grabbed him and pulled him in, and he heard him say, "Don't worry, it's All right". He knew it wasn't, don't go in the lift was the strict rule; he tried to protest but fell into a fit of coughing and was aware that the lift door had closed, and it was already on its way down. He pulled himself into a sitting position alongside the door. His rescuer was behind him, he managed a swift glance at him through the smoke. Though indistinct the figure of the young man seemed familiar, but he had no time to ponder why that was as his coughing overpowered him and then he must have passed out.

Moments later the light out of sight above his head shone "G", the lift jolted to a stop and hands reached in and he came to as they grabbed him, pulled him out and several figures held him upright and frogmarched him outside onto a patch of grass. He gulped fresh air and at once posed a question to the fireman holding him.

"Where's the other chap. In the lift. Is he okay?" He still had a vague feeling that he knew the man.

"No one else in there," said the fireman, "and you're lucky to be alive, don't you know never to get in lift when there's a fire?"

"There were explosions, I might well be dead if I hadn't," he said. Then he realised where he had seen the face he glimpsed in the lift before. The figure had said, "Don't worry, it's All right" and he realised that he had not only been talking about the safety of the lift, but he had also been talking about the operating theatre.

No hard feelings.

I guess not going in a lift when there is a fire remains good advice, even if there are occasional exceptions, besides, you cannot always rely on unexpected help.

A peaceful life

Like so many such things, it was a tedious and complex business: the form ran to 29 pages and a virtually book-sized pack of guidelines and instructions accompanied it. He had laboured long and hard over the application. It would, he was told, get him a benefit that would make all the difference to his somewhat frugal life. Many questions demanded that he look things up, what was his national insurance number for goodness sake? He could never remember such things, or the many passwords that a computer driven life seemed to demand for that matter. His computer might be old, but everything new he did on it seemed to demand a new password, and he was always prompted to make it "strong", ideally including numerals or words that made no sense. How could he ever remember, say, Flumuxy263 or 274Jobodd? Maybe he should select something funny; he remembered the story of the man who, asked for an eight-character password, selected Snow White and the seven dwarfs, but imagine typing that in every time. Urrgh, no.

Some of the form wasn't clear, it was full of typical government ambiguity and gobbledegook, and he had spent a long time on the phone to clarify matters. Well actually he had spent about two minutes on the phone clarifying matters, but getting though, now that *had* taken time, great long dollops of time and not pleasantly spent either. The first number listed on the form simply referred him to another. The second had three separate levels of push-this-push-that options, and it took half an hour to get through it; then he was cut off – twice that happened. Third time lucky, but the total time it all took was lengthy. It also involved much mandatory listening to music – the musical equivocal of reading "A to C" in the telephone directory it seemed – as well as the option pushing. And he longed for a return to the days when "Greensleeves" was the music of choice. This line favoured some screeching pop. In the end the lady he spoke to was quite helpful, she clarified what their labyrinthine and inadequate description made it necessary to check, and he completed the details and sent off the application, posting it recorded delivery, on a Thursday.

The phone horror repeated as he chased it up regularly with the Department, being told simply and more than once that "he had to allow more time". Weeks passed. Nothing happened. No reply, not even an acknowledgement. Finally, he phoned one more time and demanded to speak to a supervisor. He demanded an explanation. He demanded to know what was going on. And he must have demanded politely because he actually got through to someone: a real live person, though he would not give his name and his supervisory status was thus not guaranteed.

The office was as bright and cheerful as grey metal government-issue desks and furniture and pale magnolia painted walls can make it. In other words, it was about as dreary as the kind of railway station waiting room closed down long ago by Dr Beeching. There was (isn't there always in such offices?) a solitary rubber plant, though it had clearly not been watered for a while and drooped as if dejected and on the edge of extinction. Several people were in evidence, one man sat reading a newspaper next to two women chatting and eating sandwiches. A second man was sitting at one of the desks playing a computer game.

It was a peaceful scene, then the telephone rang on Norman's desk.

He let it ring several times while he parked the spaceship with which he was busy combating on screen invading aliens, then, his peace interrupted, he grudgingly picked up, answering with a terse, "yes". He listened for a few moments, raising an eyebrow at his colleagues that seemed to say, "Why don't they just leave us in peace?" then replied.

"Well, your form is here somewhere I'm sure, but you need to appreciate how these things work. We just can't be doing with getting everything done instantly, you know, if we were that efficient, we would certainly be in line for cuts. I might lose my job, and besides it would do you no good at all, you would be checking up on half a department in no time, and calls would take even longer to be answered. Anyway, the fact is that even with endless cups of tea, computer games and surfing the internet – and Julian is brilliant at that, even if he is in danger of going blind – things here are still getting done, well, too fast.

Hang on. Bear with me, here's the thing: you see to make things right, we set up the Losing Things Department to put a bit of a delay on matters. We got extra funding for it too, not so much, but sufficient to finance several additional people, a range of filing cabinets and a job lot of cobwebs. The place looks like a genuine old-fashioned archive.

The idea was that we would have two departments, the Losing Things one and a Finding Things one, working pretty much in parallel, but funding sort of dried up in the credit crunch. The Finding Things department was delayed, still is, and, well, to be honest there is now something of a backlog. Currently the Losing Things Department is having to find things as well as delay them and they are not equipped for that, really they're not, they don't have the resources, the people or the training; or the nous if we are truthful.

With hindsight it would obviously have been better to set up the two departments at the same time. Bad decision that, very bad, virtually a disaster, I say. But there you are, that's how it is. So, apologies, I am sure your application will come to light soon, it is only eight weeks to date after all, isn't it? Yes, I suppose that is quite a long time, but wait, there is some good news – given the current situation we have a further new reorganisation under way. Very soon a new department will be up and running and then things will be much, much better. What's that you ask? Sorry, of course, it's the Lost Things Ombudsman department. Their remit will be to investigate things that the Losing Things Department appears to have lost for rather *too* long. That will be a great help, certainly until the Finding Things Department materialises, it may even get our overall processing speed set about right. Yes, it will be up and running quite soon, very soon in fact, the current plan is to have it fully operational next year... hopefully by December. Dependent on funding, of course, and staffing... and, well realistically these things do take time, you know.

Never mind, be assured the progress of these developments is well advanced; once the proposal documents get out of the Losing Things Department and onto the head of administration's desk, we will be on our way, though actual implementation might have to wait for the setup of the Finding Things Department. Which might come first is still a little uncertain. It's just one busy round here you know.

But what about your application, you say? Yes, well,

let's see, it might help if you were to send a copy. Yes, of course, all 29 pages. Tell you what, you could send it direct to the Losing Things Department; that at least would bypass the wait in here while we decided when to send it on to them. Once you've done that, call us again in, say, six weeks – no make it seven. I'll be on holiday then, but someone will speak to you I'm sure, the Losing Things Department is nothing if not efficient. One more thing, when you address the duplicate make sure you quote the correct reference, I'll give you a TLA, that's a Things Lost Again reference number. Do you have a pen? Right, take it down carefully, one wrong digit and it won't even reach the Losing Things Department and that won't help you at all now, will it? At best it might then end up in the Now Past Retrieving section and I have to admit that they are always *glacially* slow. Anyway, here we go, careful now there are 21 digits: ready... 2, 8, 7..."

Conscious that the call was going on and on and disturbing his colleagues, he moved his finger just a fraction.

Brrrrrrrr... he heard the dialling tone return as he put the phone down and called across to his colleague.

"Finished with the newspaper yet mate, I seem to have inadvertently cut this guy off. What a shame. Still peace returns, eh."

*

In a small living room, many miles away things are far from peaceful: the sound of a telephone thrown through glass and a man's shout of rage is sufficiently loud to have a neighbour several doors away dial 999.

Never has there been a time when more people seem to have more hassle with their contact with government and large organization. Almost everyone I know always seems to have some such lengthy and frustrating saga on the go – and as soon as one is resolved another takes its place. My own most recent was online: two hours of my life that I will never get back spent completing a form after British Airways (this name crops up a lot I find) cancelled a flight and stranded me for seven hours. A form it seemed to me that was specifically designed to put all thoughts of seeking compensation out of your mind. The inspiration for "A peaceful life" (another piece that won a competition place) is all around, though telephone contact provided the most appropriate basis here. I have a feeling I am referring to the sort of thoughts many people have had in such circumstances.

A lucky encounter

Danny stared into his mug of tea and regretted making the bet so much. He enjoyed his job; he took pride in it and was getting better and better at it. Despite having passed The Knowledge as it was called almost a year ago, the unique community that made up London's Black Cab drivers still regarded him as a newcomer; indeed, they would doubtless do so for a while yet. There was still much he had to learn: just today he had got lost in a warren of streets off Tottenham Court Road, albeit only for a minute or two. He had said nothing to his passenger, a snooty business type who had spoken on his mobile phone throughout the entire journey, though he was soon back on track, his passenger none the wiser.

He had fallen into the habit of taking a break each day in one of the few remaining cabbies' rest-stops, a small building that looked like an overlarge garden shed raised a few feet off the ground. Here he was able to ask more experienced drivers the occasional question and listen to their tales as he rested for a few minutes and took in the cabbies' traditional fuel: strong tea. He liked going there, they were a good lot, some had now become mates and he enjoyed the cheery welcome and the banter amongst whatever group was there; but he still shouldn't have made the bet. The chances of his winning were minimal, and he had seen the look one or two of the old timers had given him: an eyebrow firmly raised to show they clearly thought he was pushing his luck.

He'd fallen a bit silent after that. Then he finished his tea and, trying to be cheery, stood up and made some comment about having to get on.

"Maybe see you tomorrow," said Joe, grinning. It was he who had mooted the bet. He was an older man, always quick to point out his greater experience and wont to see what he thought of as the youngsters as rivals, and he was someone with whom Danny seemed to cross paths regularly.

"Okay," he replied. "Bye".

Susan was still new to this celebrity business. Some of it was assuredly fun, but some of it was downright scary, like the crowds of photographers that seemed to appear from nowhere wherever she went. All of it was hard work, but on other occasions it could be boring. She was at the Connaught Rooms, a suite of function rooms off Holborn, for what her agent had described briefly over the phone as a press interview. She tried to do these things right and so she had arrived early, now she sat in reception waiting for her agent to join her, conscious that many of the people passing recognised her and looked… and looked some more. She turned her eyes away, hoping they would think they were mistaken, that it wasn't *the* Susan Hampson. Despite this, already one person had asked for her autograph.

She fumbled in her bag for a mint, her mouth was dry, and she could murder a cup of tea. Suddenly she was conscious of someone standing over her. She looked up to see a young man dressed in jeans, a checked shirt and a padded waistcoat jacket. He had an envelope in his hand and a London taxi drivers' badge swinging from around his neck. She recognised the badge at once. Her father was a cabbie or had been – he was now retired and living happily by the sea in the bungalow she had bought him with some of the proceeds that flowed in when that first disc had topped the charts.

"Susan Hampson?"

There was clearly a question mark at the end of what he said even though his face made it perfectly clear that he knew exactly who she was. Danny, who had been hailed in Oxford Street by a man who had given him a twenty-pound note and told him to deliver the envelope, had not expected this, even having seen the name on the envelope. It really was her. She nodded and he handed it over.

"This is for you," he said, still clearly besotted. She took the envelope and tore it open. The message from her agent was brief to the point of abruptness: "Interview being rearranged – go home in the taxi – call you this afternoon". What a pain. She looked up and saw the cabby was waiting.

"Okay," she said. "Thanks for that. Can you take me to Islington?"

"Sure, of course."

Danny couldn't believe his luck Susan – Suzy – Hampson in *his* cab. Wow. And again, wow.

He led her outside to the cab, which was parked just a few steps beyond the entrance. He opened the passenger door for her, and, in a burst of unaccustomed social bravery, he said, "You are *the* Suzy Hampson, aren't you?"

"Yes, I suppose I am," she smiled now, relaxing as the worry of the impending interview departed and she could look forward to a quiet morning back at home. She actually enjoyed the exclamation that followed.

"That's f – f – antastic," he said, adding, "sorry, it's a pleasure to see you, I just love you". He shut the passenger door and climbed into the cab, and she smiled again.

"So, what are up to?" he asked, an idea taking root in his mind.

"A cancelled interview", she said to his face in the mirror, "bit of a relief really, I hate all that – I'd much rather just chat to ordinary people. My dad was a cabbie like you". She saw him nod at that.

Danny put the cab in gear and pulled away from the kerb, he executed a neat U turn and headed for Holborn en route to Islington. After a little way, his bravery unaccountably increased.

"Would you, I wonder, would you do me a favour?" he said.

"I can sign an autograph for you if you like." Her voice sounded from the back.

"It's not that," he said, "Well, actually, yes, please, but ..."

He pulled into the kerb and stopped.

"I'll switch the meter off," he said, "Just give me a moment to explain". She lent forward towards the open window between them.

Ten minutes later he pushed the door of his favourite cabbies' rest-room open and shouted above the chatter.

"Shut up for a moment, guys, I've a visitor for you".

He ushered Suzy into the tiny room. She beamed at the aghast faces ranged round her and said "So, what do I have to do to get a cup of tea round here?"

In the last six months she had become the nation's sweetheart. Everyone recognised her; even Joe who professed never to take his radio off BBC Radio 4 and always said pop music was "the devil's work". His face registered considerable surprise.

Somehow, she instantly felt at ease. Danny went to the kettle. They all chatted, they drank tea and, having said she was hungry, someone found some chocolate digestives and she ate half a dozen explaining that she had left home that morning without breakfast. She signed autographs for them all and posed kissing

Danny's cheek for a selfie photo on his phone. Time passed quickly and suddenly realising this she apologised saying, "Sorry, I really must get back".

Amidst the protests that followed, Danny showed her out and back to his cab. They drove on and finally he got out and opened the rear door for her in the small mews in Islington to where she had directed him.

"Thanks so much. You're an absolute star," he said, "that made our day; besides I've never had anyone famous in my cab before and you, well ... who better?"

"No problem," she replied, "but you should have told me about the bet – Joe told me while you made the tea, first one this year to have someone really famous in their cab, eh – all that guff when you first asked about getting a photo for your granny. Really! You did have me hooked but I'd have gone for the bet too, you know, remember I said my dad was a cabbie." Danny looked sheepish, thinking that if she hadn't told him that then he'd never have had the nerve to ask her to come for a cuppa.

"Joe's a bit of a rival," he said, "and I thought you'd refuse the bet business, but I guess I should've been honest – though truthfully granny will love the photo."

Danny had insisted on not switching on the taxi meter on the drive to her home, saying, "It's on the house", but as Suzy stood with him at the kerb, she insisted on paying for her journey, and for the second time that day Danny found himself getting a twenty-pound note and being told to keep the change.

"Have this too," she said pulling a CD out of her bag, her signature already showing across the stunning photo on the cover. She leant into the cab and gave him a kiss him on the cheek, turned to unlock her front door and disappeared inside with a final wave and a smile.

What a day, he thought; especially that kiss, what would a photo of that be worth he wondered? Then he remembered the selfie. He looked forward to his break tomorrow... especially as he still had to collect the tenner Joe now owed him.

He engaged first gear, switching on the radio as he pulled away from the kerb. A few minutes later Suzy's voice flooded the cab and he smiled to himself.

I have a family member who is a London cabbie, and I know they do sometimes get both someone famous in the back and have interesting, surprising or funny tales to tell as a result. Many a celebrity would not go this far to please a fan, but some would, so inventing one who does for "A lucky encounter" seems to me to be credible.

Holiday work

Julie gazed into his eyes and said, "Yes, I'd like that."

She had had something of a bad year, indeed, to say that even time on a sun kissed beach in Thailand had been struggling to make up for it was a gross understatement. What had made her think that sitting alone by a pool even in perfect weather and wonderful surroundings would make everything better, she wondered? But maybe her friend Abigail had been right, insisting that she take a break. She took a sip of her cold beer, smiled at the man across the table as she found her mind wandering back a year or so.

She and her husband had had a nice life, good jobs, a pleasant home and enough money to live comfortably. She thought they were happy, until she came home one day to find suitcases stacked in the hall and John telling her he was leaving her for someone else. He wouldn't even discuss it; a taxi drew up outside and he was gone. He had everything organised: an envelope left on the hall table contained divorce papers. There was still a lot of sorting out to do. The house had to be sold and the money shared. She now lived in an apartment; it wasn't the same. She had lost herself in work, but she was still miserable. She felt a failure. Seven years of marriage had led nowhere. Then she'd met Frank. In the supermarket of all places. Really, how likely was that? She thought that he was to be her salvation, she thought they had a future together. She thought it was love and told herself how lucky she was.

"You're miles away, what are you thinking?" Simon's voice interrupted her rambling thoughts.

"Sorry," she replied hastily, "it's just that view, its mesmerizing." They both gazed along the long beach as waves rolled in with a comforting crunch against the white sand. She added quickly, "you suggested lunch, where shall we go?" After a brief discussion they walked along the sand towards a small beach café. Simon held her hand.

Frank had hit her. What seemed like salvation had proved illusory and even her normal optimism began to flag. Now, after all that, she could hardly believe a holiday romance, was that what this was she wondered, was lifting her spirits and making her think long term again. So quickly. Maybe this time. She had met Simon at the bar by the pool. They had talked, seemed to hit it off, and talked some more, long into the night. He was tall and good looking with close cropped brown hair and an easy manner. But he had told her little about himself. He was "between jobs," he was wondering "whether to stay in Thailand for a while," he "had looked at one or two villas with a view to renting." She wanted to know more, but for the moment she was content just to have a likeable lunch companion and wondered if she should allow it to be more than that.

Later, when they parted after an afternoon by the pool and supper at the same beach restaurant, he had lent forward and kissed her. She would have to decide how much further this went. Back in her room, she switched on a small tablet. She had a quick look at the BBC news app and decided that nothing of much importance was happening at home, then clicked on her email. Amongst a number of circulars was a message from her friend Abigail wanting to know how she was; there was also a message from a colleague at work. Julie worked as a policewoman and the message contained a news item about a fraudster. A Richard Williams had evidently disappeared from the city bank where he held a senior position taking eight million pounds with him. "Bloody bankers," she whispered under her breath, but she wondered why on Earth she had been sent it. She was on holiday, for goodness sake. Then she saw her colleague had ended her brief message by saying: *it's reckoned he may be holed up in Thailand, keep your eyes peeled, maybe you can up your arrest rate! Have a good holiday.*

Yes, she thought, like she was likely to meet a major crook walking along the beach. What were the chances of that? The email had an attachment, and clicking on that she found a photograph. She opened it up to discover that sure enough she had not just met said Richard Williams on the beach – she had just kissed the bugger goodnight.

Even though nothing more had happened she cried herself to sleep that night: another possible romance had bitten the dust – could things get any worse she wondered? In the morning things got worse. She had arranged to meet the man she knew as Simon for breakfast. There was no mistake, he had cut his hair short, but the face clearly confirmed the fact that she had been about to get into bed with a crook; literally. She felt sick, hadn't life thrown enough at her recently?

"You're very quiet," he said, cutting fresh pineapple on the plate in front of him while she stared into her coffee.

"Yes, sorry, not feeling too well. I'm going to get a taxi to the town and go to a pharmacy. See you by the pool later maybe, okay." She refused all his attempts to accompany her, saying she needed to be on her own and shake off a headache. Later she joined him by the pool and explained she was going to lie down in her room for a while.

"Just the heat, I expect," she said. "I'll find you

later."

The phone summoned her to Reception about six in the evening. Two uniformed Thai policemen met her, alongside a man seemingly from England. He introduced himself as Detective Inspector James Walters and explained that they had firm evidence that Richard Williams had fled to Thailand and so he had been sent there to liaise with the local authorities. This meant that he had already been only three hour's drive away in Bangkok when she had contacted the police. They would not let her go with them as they headed for the pool bar, where she suggested they would probably find the fugitive. But as she sat in Reception, contemplating a lucky escape, she saw them escorting him out to a waiting police car; the fugitive with his head down and his hands handcuffed. As they drew level with her James Walters left the group and came over, she stood up and he extended his hand and shook hers.

"You did very well Julie," he said. "Well spotted."

He was still holding her hand as he smiled and added: "I must buy you dinner tonight. I'll wrap this up and see you at eight o'clock. Must go now."

He did not wait for a reply, seemingly confident that she would agree. Later over dinner she found her optimism kicking in again as his engaging smile seemed to hold the possibility of a whole new beginning. Maybe, now at last, things were on the up.

I have visited Thailand many times over the years (sufficient that one of my travel books, "Smile because it happened", relates solely to the land of smiles). Because of this I tend to go there whenever a story needs a holiday or a beach setting. I guess "Holiday work" could equally be in South America, though discovery is more likely in this scenario, I think.

Down the garden path

There was a good deal Joyce was not sure about these days. Was it Wednesday or Thursday? Did she have anything planned for the day? Who would she see? If anyone; she seemed to see fewer and fewer people these days and, of course, she did not get out and about like she used to do. She used to go to London every day, up early, off to the station and a day spent in the offices of a large insurance company in the City. She was quite high-powered in those days. At home too she and Graham used to do so much, always out to the cinema, the theatre or just to see friends. She did miss Graham, she missed him so much.

She dressed slowly, thinking that there was no other way to do it these days, pulling on trousers with an elasticated waist and donning a matching cardigan that had been a present at Christmas. She was sitting at the kitchen table with a slice of toast and a tray with various medicines and a glass of water on it in front of her when the doorbell rang. Chloe. It was her day to visit she realised; it must be Wednesday. She began to get up.

"Hi there Joyce." Chloe had used her key and was already in the house, as she came through the kitchen door smiling broadly, wearing a yellow tabard and with her unruly hair in an arrangement that barely succeeded in taming it, she saw Joyce slowly rising from her seat.

"Oh, don't get up, you know I have a key, I just rang the bell to let you know I was coming in, did you remember I was coming today?"

Joyce had not remembered but she replied, "Yes, of course, it's Wednesday, you come every Wednesday." Chloe smiled a smile that said caring with a capital C.

"Have you taken your medicines yet?" Chloe asked, continuing brightly, "come on, let me help."

She counted out the pills from a plastic box divided into compartments indicating the time and the day they were due to be taken and passed Joyce a glass of water. She visited every week and did a range of chores Joyce could no longer cope with so easily since her health deteriorated. She managed very well, she was well into her eighties after all, but a helping hand was appreciated and that was what Chloe saw herself as.

"I'm going to start with the bedroom first today," she said, "I will change the bedsheets and then clean the bathroom – why don't I make you another cup of tea and you can sit outside while I get on? It's a lovely morning and the forecast on the news was good."

Joyce smiled and nodded. The garden. She so loved her garden. Graham had worked hard at it. It was very bare years back when they bought the house, but he had planted a range of plants, including shrubs and trees, creating a maze of small paths and areas decorated by a plethora of colours. It was a place to relax and a place to walk, many family events had taken place there over the years and she remembered several generations of hide and seek taking place around its different areas. Once she had walked past young Jonathan hidden above her in a tree so many times before a slight noise had made her look up. She smiled inwardly at the recollection.

"Yes, the garden would be lovely," she said. She got up, took her stick from alongside her chair and as she turned Chloe opened the back door and then guided her, just a little, as they went out. Immediately outside the door was an old oak bench. It had been in the family for many years, it was well weathered and very comfortable, or it was with the right cushion. Chloe slipped the cushion, kept just inside the back door, onto the seat as Joyce sat down.

"Will you be okay? I'll pop back in a half an hour or so when I have done the first jobs." She returned moments later and put Joyce's tea down on the table alongside the chair.

"That's fine, thank you so much." Joyce watched her go back into the house. She very much appreciated Chloe's visits and knew that she could probably not live so independently without some such help.

She took a sip of tea then got up slowly. She wasn't immobile and, even though she could not go too far, she could still manage the garden. It was not so big. Holding her stick firmly she set off down the path. The surface was brick and a little uneven, but Joyce knew it well and walked slowly but steadily. At the end of the path, she ducked through an arch in the hedge that ran across the garden and was into an area with a small square lawn surrounded by borders brimming with plants of a variety of hues. Further on the path was gravel, not so easy to navigate and she gripped her stick tightly as she went along. There was a loop she could walk around; she would emerge back near the house along a path on the other side of the garden and should be back in her chair before Chloe came back out to check on her. She suspected Chloe would worry if she walked too far. Joyce could hear her voice, "Just sit quietly, the sun's warm today, can I get you a book or anything?" But Joyce liked to see the garden, Graham had loved it too. She remembered good times spent in it together. Dear Graham, she did miss him. But the garden was still kept nice, she was very lucky and walking in it made her feel closer to him.

When Chloe came out a little later, she found Joyce still

sitting comfortably on the bench, the sun warm enough to make it a nice spot.

"Let's get you safe inside again before I leave," she said. Joyce got up and allowed Chloe to help her up the step and back into the house. Chloe made more tea and they sat and chatted for a while – Chloe updated her about her two children, about a coming school trip, a camping expedition: the school do well with such things Chloe explained while bemoaning how much any planned outing always seemed to cost. There was a birthday coming up soon too: James would be eight on the 22nd. Joyce listened, of course, she loved Chloe's visits and tried to follow her news week by week. But she found her mind wandering a bit too, being able to get around the garden was her greatest pleasure; she could still see those bulbs coming up, such a bright yellow, so pretty. Soon the sound of a car hooting outside the house interrupted Chloe's chatter.

"That will be my husband come to collect me," she said, "I'm glad you're keeping well, and I'll see you again soon, okay?"

"Fine, fine," said Joyce, with a smile, "and thank you for getting me out into the garden, I do so enjoy that."

They said their goodbyes and Chloe went out to the car, her husband would get her home, then she had another visit to make in the afternoon. Ian lent over and gave her a kiss on the cheek as she got into the passenger seat.

"Hello Chloe love, everything okay this morning?" He asked, he always took an interest in what he called her "old fogeys".

"Yes, pretty good," she replied. "I got all my jobs done. As the weather was good, Joyce sat outside for most of my visit today, she loves that, though I sometimes wonder what she finds to love about that tiny little yard."

"Down the garden path" is intended to be slightly ambiguous at the end. Is the ending sad or uplifting? Poignant is perhaps a better description.

A break by the beach

She sat comfortably by the pool beyond which she could see a wonderful view of the Andaman Sea, yet she was restless. The book she was reading was excellent, a real page turner, yet her mind kept wandering. She stopped reading, got up, stepped out into the sun from under the umbrella, dived into the pool and swam a few lengths, reflecting on her situation as she did so. Jill and her husband had separated, but divorce seemed a long way off. He was being so unreasonable. The word fair did not seem to exist in his vocabulary. He wanted too much, and she was going to protect her business if it was the last thing she did. Besides, she thought as she wrapped a towel around herself and settled back down on the sun lounger, he was a cheating, lying rat and she owed him absolutely nothing.

She felt she deserved this holiday after months of juggling various wrangles with her ex while still running the successful recruitment agency she had founded ten years ago. Of that she was certain. But even here she had trouble relaxing. Sitting alone she people-watched her fellow resort guests. She gave names to those that struck her as odd in some way. There was the middle-aged man with the disapproving look she christened Red Hat, so called from the baseball cap that never left his head. He always sat on an upright chair and seemed to do nothing but organise the posse of people he appeared to be holidaying with, he looked the part too: officious, oh so officious; she imagined him in some government office saying, "The computer says no" and brooking no argument. He organised a different member of his group to use towels to reserve eight sun loungers by the pool every morning, adding copies of old magazines abandoned at the resort so long ago some contained articles about Britain *joining* the European Union. She could see this happening from her room window, though it had taken her two days to discover that whoever did it went out before dawn broke. They had to search the pool boys' area using the torches on their mobile phones to find the necessary towels. Then the chairs sat empty for hours, they never appeared until nearly midday; very much not her kind of people.

Then there was the one she called prison warder. She was huge, always wore a tee shirt and huge, long baggy shorts, both black like her close-cut hair, and who had every visible stretch of sagging flesh covered in garish tattoos. Another woman nearly twice the size of the warden she named tsunami. Everyone else stood back as she entered the pool. And who knew that they even made bikinis in such a size. Gross. Some things in life, Jill concluded, were just inexplicable. Then there was Eating Machine, Preener, Lecher and a screeching kid who Jill thought had a distinctly demonic look to him. He could turn his head right round. She was sure of it, though he didn't do it when anyone could see. Of course not. Inevitably she christened him Damian. Thank goodness for the adults' only pool she thought.

The biggest mystery was a man she called Xman. Attractive, in his late thirties, he swam well and was clearly fit; in both senses of the word thought Jill. But there was something sinister about him, of that Jill was certain. A spy? A crook? She was not sure, but she was suspicious. She felt something bad lurking. She was sure something about him was not right. She might settle on a specific thought at some point, but meantime he was an enigma.

Time passed and Jill usually found herself having a drink at a beach bar at the end of the evening when it was Happy Hour – two Margaritas for the price of one helped put her horrid ex to the back of her mind. She had found a short cut from the bar to her room first going along the beach, then cutting through the huge gardens surrounding the resort and heading back towards the hotel.

As she took this route a few days into her stay, she got lost. The gardens were lush with tropical vegetation and the paths narrow. As she retraced her steps, she heard voices. It was Xman, she could just see him through the thick greenery, his back was to her, and he appeared to be arguing with another man who was barely visible. But she saw all too clearly what happened next, and it made her shrink back into the bushes stifling a gasp. Xman had pulled a knife and stabbed the other man who he held for a moment and then lowered to the ground and rolled off the path. Jill was terrified and shrank back further. What if he had seen her? A witness might well be disposed of as ruthlessly as the way the first killing had been executed. Xman looked around carefully and then moved away from both the body and Jill. She could hardly believe what had happened, though she allowed herself to dwell on how right her instincts had been. Her suspicions that he was a wrong'un were spot on. She took a few steps forward, letting out a breath she had not realised she was holding as she did so. She did not recognise the man who lay half concealed in the dense garden, but he was assuredly dead. She hurried past the body, then slowed, she did not want to run into the assassin.

Jill continued to walk slowly back to the poolside and sat down, lay back and closed her eyes. What was she to do? She should report it, of course she must, but how could it be proved and if Xman then went unrestrained how safe was she? She let the thought buzz round for a few moments and when she opened her eyes the first thing she saw was the killer. Lying on the sun bed next to her. He knew she had seen him kill she thought, he knew. But he just smiled and made a comment about the beach. Before she knew it, they were chatting – it was bizarre. He asked her why she was staying on her own and she prattled on about her ex though becoming more uneasy by the moment. What if he had seen her?

"And you," she said, "you're here alone too?" He looked at her long and hard, a look that emphasised the side of him that had made Jill suspicious earlier that there was something not right about him.

"Yes, just a few days relaxation linked to a little business I had nearby... but you know all about that don't you?" He replied. He knew, he had seen her and what she had witnessed was not just an argument that got out of hand, it had been planned, he called it business, he must... she became aware he was speaking again.

"You and me need to have a bit of a chat, don't we?" He said, his voice low and menacing.

What could she do? It seemed clear he aimed to kill her too. Few people remained at the pool at this hour, and no one was watching them. She found herself speaking, her voice shaky.

"I think I know what you mean by that," she said, and she started to get up.But he motioned her not to move and allowed her to see the knife he held concealed from others by his side. She reckoned she might only have moments and she knew she had to do something. Then an idea struck her, it arrived fully formed in her brain. Of course. Maybe there was a way. She held up her hand in what looked like a calming gesture, and she spoke more confidently now and yet softly so that only he could hear:

"Hang on. We are both businesspeople aren't we – so I have a proposition for you. Tell me, how much would it cost me to have you kill my husband?" The man smiled.

One thing leads to another. As I have said I have put other characters on a beach in Thailand and writing about one can lead to thoughts about something different in the same setting. I guess I just like thinking about beaches in Thailand.

The Bucket List

In two short weeks he would get to the end of the list. But what next? Bucket lists have something of a morbid aspect, his friend Brian had told him when he had first mooted the idea of compiling one more than a year back, adding that he himself was way too young to be thinking of such things. But a session in the pub had him warming to the idea when Mark had explained more. The two men had been friends for many years and regularly met for lunch on Saturdays while their wives disappeared to indulge in what Brian described only as "something girly". This usually meant a shopping expedition.

"What exactly constitutes a bucket list?" Brian had asked, adding quickly, "if you put 'Bucket list' into Google you get masses of hits and many of those are headed '1000 things to put on your bucket list' – no one would ever have time for that".

"I guess not," said Mark.

"Anyway, I propose to give it a go," continued Mark, "I thought twenty was a nice round number for my purposes and anyway some of the things you hear of people listing I wouldn't *want* to do, not in a million years."

They both agreed that ruled out the dangers of sky diving and bungee jumping for a start; they agreed about that as the beer arrived and they moved from the bar to a table to await their food.

Mark continued the conversation: "You know, some

things seem a very attractive proposition but if, or when, you do them, they just prove disappointing. Take cars. For years I lusted after a Morgan, you know the classic sports car, then I met someone who had one and was offered a ride. Oh, it was so disappointing. They look a million dollars, but they are so, *so* uncomfortable! Low, hard, and, well that turned out to be a day of very great disappointment I can tell you. I shall have to give all this some serious thought." He took a sip of beer and repeated: "Yes indeed, very serious thought."

Brian nodded. "One suggestion," he said, "I think the things you list have to be possible. Realistically you need to accept that you will never actually sleep with Jennifer Lawrence, and you are not going to go to travel to the Moon, to Mars or even into orbit. Never mind, I suggest you start really big with travel round the world." He took a sip of ale after volunteering something he would certainly like to do if time and money were no limit.

"Good idea," replied his friend, "a special trip is surely high on the list, but do I put things like visit Hong Kong, climb the Empire State Building and have a cuppa in a Japanese Tea House down as well or does Travel round the world cover them all and still count as one on the list?"

"Well, you might not fulfil everything like that on a single trip, a single circumnavigation," said Brian, "you'd be away forever. Though I guess it depends on whether a list of twenty lets you get in everything you want to do."

The possibilities grew as they chatted and, getting serious about the idea, Mark purloined paper and pen from one of the bar staff and began writing a list. Some things he was sure about, the round the world trip for one and he had always wanted to drive a racetrack.

"Two steak pies?" A waitress hovered over them

clutching two plates. They nodded and she put them on the table and, disappearing, returned a moment later with cutlery. They tucked in. Then, moments later Mark spoke up again.

"Wait a minute." Mark put his knife and fork down, took a sip of beer and explained: "I can't do this alone," he said, "certainly I can't just disappear round the world, I'd want Tracy to come with me." Tracy was his wife of almost twenty years; omitting her would no doubt hasten the moment of Mark's death; and would likely make it a painful one. "I guess I'll have to consult, she doesn't like heights so that might rule out the Empire State Building. Another thing: you must do some of these things with me, Brian, are you up for a track driving day? You know what, this may all be a bit more complicated than I thought." His face adopted a serious expression as he folded the paper and put it in his pocket, with Brian nodding enthusiastically at the racetrack idea. Then they talked of other things for a while as they finished lunch.

"Let me know how the list turns out." Brian requested as they left the pub and went their separate ways. Mark promised to do so and when they met for their next weekly lunch Mark handed him a neatly typed list numbered from 1 to 20.

"It's done," he said, adding to the barman, "two pints of Doom Bar please".

The list was in two parts: number one was Travel round the world, followed by several items that clearly could only be fulfilled by doing just that. Then there were a few other separate items including driving a racing car and taking a hot air balloon ride.

"Tracy won't do the balloon trip," said Mark, "but she has some items of her own that I won't take part in – I have no wish to ride on an elephant, thank you very much. Some things need details filling in, for instance there is a balloon trip you can do in Burma that sounds special; one to do during the round the world trip perhaps. And I have made a start, just one simple thing, but something I have never ever done before."

In due course a year had passed since the subject first came up and when they next met in the pub Brian, who had not only followed his friend's progress but been involved in some of his exploits, immediately asked: "You've reached the end of that list, I know, so now what?"

Mark grinned. "Well, yes, I have. All great fun it was too, so I guess I'll just have to start another list, won't I? And, you know what, when I think back, I will never know why I did it, I'd not done it before and I've not done it since, never even been tempted – yet it was number one on the list and I couldn't have experienced any of the rest if I hadn't bought that lottery ticket!"

I am not sure what made me think of the core idea in this one for I have never been a gambler, however a tale of out and out good fortune is nice sometimes, I think.

Sometimes only a letter will do

Dear Paul

I say Paul, but I hope there are not too many people named Paul there, though possibly in your case Paul is a kind of nom de plume and your real name is Soli Patel; your accent seemed more Bombay than Balham to me. Sorry Mumbai now, isn't it? Anyway, the person I want is the Paul I spoke to this morning after dialling your 08cost-a-fortune number, pressing option 2 at the first level, option 3 at the second and option 5 at the third, followed by being put on hold for 25 minutes as you were *so* busy looking after other happy customers who had got through ahead of me. Or drinking coffee, or watching the cricket, which I'm told is mighty important where you are. Mind you, 25 minutes it may have been, but I have never heard a nicer version of The Four Seasons, or heard it so often for that matter, so thank you for that. Thanks too for taking the trouble to record my every word when we did speak, you must be up to your armpits in tapes by now, but – never mind – good record-keeping is the sign of a tidy mind. So that's a good sign, though frankly nothing, but nothing at all, else is.

Anyway it's the Paul I finally got through to at 10 am this morning that I want, the one who started by telling me that my call was important to him and then told me that the record showed that you already know all about my broadband connection being down for the last month and that you had emailed me twice to tell me that it will all be up and running again soon: after you have run some tests, thought about it for a while and fitted taking further action in with all the phone calls you have to take I presume. You were less clear about what you would actually do to get things working again; and even less clear about whether I could get a refund of the money I have paid you for the period when there has been no service. Though, as you will appreciate, there still is no service, so perhaps a refund should wait until you have done whatever it is you are going to do, and I finally have a service again – if I ever do.

Incidentally, highly trained I am sure you are and a fully paid-up member of the Institute of Customer Dissatisfaction too, I'll be bound, but I wonder if you have actually quite got the hang of this broadband business. Broadband is what I use to connect me to the Internet; it's a wireless world now you know and most of us can't manage without it – we use it every day, several times a day if you count my buying and selling on Amazon and Gran's regular bingo and poker sessions. It is also what I use to access my email – so, when you know my connection is as disconnected as Philip Scofield is from that tedious morning television programme (sorry, you may not follow such bizarre antics in India), what in the name of all that's digital is the use of sending me an email to tell me you are going to mend it? What kind of blithering, brain-dead, unthinking idiot can think that is a good idea, much less actually do it twice (you told me you sent it again when you got no reply) – three weeks ago – rather than telephoning me or writing a letter? Was it you? Is it "policy"? Do you do it to everyone? No, don't tell me, I don't want to know. For future reference, please bear in mind that *I can't receive email* – that's the problem, that's what I am trying to get you to correct. My friend next door is already upset with me nipping in to use their computer every five minutes.

What I do want to know – and soon – is what, if anything, is happening and when exactly something will be done to fix things. Let me be clear, I know you may have trouble with English and my non-existent Hindi certainly allows no alternative, but "fix things" means getting the connection working again and emails filling my eager in-box to the brim, even if a lot of them are spam (though if it's you who send me those – please stop). It does not mean emailing me something I can't see without a trip down the road, it does not mean ignoring me and putting this letter in a pending pile the height of your blessed Himalayas, it does not mean passing it to another department, especially not the "if you can't fix it, what makes you think we can" department, and it assuredly does *not* mean leaving it until I get fed up waiting and telephone again. I dread subjecting myself again to the horrors of your labyrinthine telephone system. Even a promise of hearing a new piece of music will not persuade me to do that again.

Remember that I have now spoken to you or one of your colleagues 27 times over the last month. Each time I am assured that "all will be well soon", each time a disembodied voice assures me that "my call is important" and each time I am cut off in the middle and have to redial – often dozens of times as the line is often engaged. I think I have now spent a total of 20 hours on the phone to you in a so far vain attempt to sort this matter out – that's almost a whole day, damnit; I'm a busy man, in fact that's almost as long as the last break I took from work.

Anyway Paul, I am hoping that with this letter we can skip all the option selection, holding on and annoying music of telephone communication. We can skip too your excuses and your platitudes and all the glib promises you make that clearly mean nothing. You won't have to spend time on hold to get this message from me: it will land right on your desk. It will be right in front of you as you clock in, and you can read it before the tea wallah comes round with the first cuppa of the morning. Of course, I'm sending it to your corporate headquarters in England, I'm blowed if I'm paying for airmail postage, and besides you refused to give me your address, so it may take some time for it to get to you out there in the sub-continent, but please, when you do get it – please, please, double please with bells on, can you get someone to nip into my local telephone exchange, if that's where the trouble lies, with a set of knitting needles or whatever is necessary and connect me up again.

This whole business is not only driving me mad, but also affecting my life, my business and my state of mind, not to mention Gran's bingo. And when it is fixed, please let me know. Ring me, go on – one quick call, you have my number – I'm sure policy says you can't ring anyone back, certainly you've never done it for me, but make an exception, go on just this once – you might even find it liberating. Remember the time difference between us, don't you dare wake me in the middle of the night and if there is no reply, ring for an ambulance (that means dialling 999 here) as I will in all likelihood have slit my wrists. And if I do that – be warned: my last will and testament will leave a significant sum to my friendly neighbourhood hit man, with instructions about torture and death and a first class return air ticket to Bombay. He'll have your name so warn any other Pauls there may be in your office as he will miss no one rather than risk you escaping.

So, the alternatives are simple: fix my wretched connection or die! I would rather you fixed it, but the pleasure of thinking of you being slowly strangled by your own phone line grows more appealing by the minute. I await your reply.

Yours very sincerely...

This letter was never sent, but I wrote this, albeit somewhat exaggerated, piece during a long, frustrating period when my own broadband really did cease to work. When my broadband was finally reconnected, the charge for the time during which it was out was waived and I was paid £100.00 "for your inconvenience". But, my goodness, it took some time and many frustrating communications. This particular letter was never sent, as I say, so Paul is no doubt still going about his business, unaware of just how near he came to an untimely death. If you ever hear from him – beware.

An early morning proposal

Someone once said that: *If God had intended us to fly, he would never have given us the railways.* The comment has some merit, a rail journey, especially when there is no time pressure, can be a delight and no train provides more delight than the famous Orient Express. This is well known in Europe, less so in Southeast Asia where what is there called The Eastern & Oriental Express travels regularly from Singapore through Malaysia and on along the peninsula north into Thailand, the capital Bangkok and beyond.

Despite the word express in its name, for the most part it is a leisurely journey and travelling on it is a special and luxurious treat, indeed much of what makes it so is mysterious. For instance, I wondered how on Earth they served such wonderful four course, silver service dinners out of a kitchen not much larger than a broom cupboard. Every aspect of the service is designed to spoil you. There are sights to see as you go, stops to make to investigate things further and, like so much travel, it is the people you meet who can add interest and quirkiness to the journey.

Each evening an events sheet is issued to all the passengers, itemising the highlights of the next leg of the journey. For today the schedule said, "6-40 a.m. - Cross Bukit Merah Lake". Now I normally subscribe firmly to the old maxim that, *If God had intended us to see the sunrise, he would never have made it so early in the morning.* But I was on a 1200 mile once-in-a-lifetime-luxury train journey, and I wanted to experience everything the classic journey offered.

So, I set my alarm, got up and dressed and set off along the corridor towards the rear of the train; I saw no other passenger.

Arriving at the last carriage of the train, I found the observation car was empty of passengers with only the uniformed policeman the train always carries sitting alongside the serving station. He had a pistol on his hip, but was somewhat bulky and not the alert, lean individual I would have liked to see in such a role. Besides he was sitting with his head lolling on his chest sound asleep. Later in the trip I asked him if there was ever any trouble aboard. "It's just as well I'm here," he said. "The trouble we sometimes get. Sneak thieves, rampaging bandits and the passengers, well, drunken brawls, jealous rages, and the fury of cuckolded lovers. Yes, it's just lucky I'm here to keep you all safe." In reality, I do not think he spoke very good English; all he really said was a firm "No!", coupling this with a what-an-idea kind of grin and shaking his head.

The final third of this last carriage is a viewing platform open to the elements. Passengers can stand outside with the view unencumbered even by a window, though there is a good old breeze to buffet you when the train is travelling at any speed. It seemed just the spot from which to see the promised lake at sunrise.

I went outside and stood alone on the observation deck. It was almost like having your own train. Just outside the door it was okay, but when I moved back to the rail at the rear the movement of the train made it very blustery. I retreated back inside, where one other passenger had now appeared. An American – "I'm Harry from Connecticut" – he immediately set about quizzing me as to the availability of coffee, which we agreed was due on tap here at 7 am. As if responding to his evidently dire need for wake-up fluid, a smiling waitress appeared on cue and coffee was duly served. She was a young Thai, like all the staff on the train she wore a smart uniform, in her case of brightly coloured silk, and was also strikingly beautiful. Harry sipped his coffee and immediately, and with hardly pause for a thank you, asked the girl if she was married. Surely not a question you expect to be asked at seven in the morning just as you come on duty. She looked mildly taken aback and said simply, "No". Harry offered to help. "I've got two sons back in the States, they're both good looking lads, how about you marry one of them?" He didn't wait for an answer, continuing, "You can choose, I won't influence you, I would be happy for either of them to get hitched – do you want to see a picture?" Without pause or reply he promptly produced a photograph from his wallet and passed it over. She looked appalled – were they werewolves or something I wondered – and she said, very politely I thought in the circumstances, "No, thank you". Given the level of passenger service and courtesy offered here whatever else was she to say to such an offer? She handed the photo back to Harry who turned it round so that it faced me. It showed two smiling young boys of maybe six and eight years old. He was right: they were good looking kids. "They are twenty-five and twenty-seven now," he said brightly. "And both are available". She smiled now, well a little, but clearly thought this was all a touch odd. I'm not sure that even the presumably exacting E & O staff training teaches you how to respond to a proposal of marriage, made at seven in the morning, especially when it is made on behalf of someone else. Despite this she kept her cool, stayed polite and concentrated on the coffee.

The enigmatic look Harry received made me ponder the nature of smiles in the land of smiles. True, Thai people smile a lot, but their doing so can indicate more than pleasure or amusement; it can also be a sign of embarrassment or more. I remember a Thai once telling me that there were, I think, rather more than a dozen recognisable kinds of smile in their culture. He explained that one meant that everything was one hundred percent good and that at the other end of the scale was a smile that said its owner was poised to hit you. "Of course," he said, "as a *farang* (white foreigner) you may find it difficult to tell the difference." He smiled as he told me. I wondered where on the scale the smile following the marriage proposal had been situated.

Was the sight of the lake worth the early rising? Yes, indeed. The views throughout the journey had been great, but this, the sun sparkling on the water stretching away into the distance, was spectacular and amongst the best sights of the journey. Besides, I had met Harry and enjoyed hearing his proposal; it was all part of a journey to remember.

Okay, here I am cheating, "An early morning proposal" is not fiction it is based on a real personal experience described in my book "First Class at Last!" Details of that appear in the final few pages of this book. Having shifted gear as it were, the next piece also relates to travel and is, I believe, something many readers will smile at and is likely to ring a bell in terms of flights taken in the past.

Are you sitting comfortably?

However good a holiday you have booked it is always proceeded by the small matter of getting there. Or rather the *not so small* matter of getting there. Travel any distance overseas and this will almost inevitably involve a flight. Ignoring the hassle and tedium that combine to create the horror of the typical airport experience, what about the plane? The airlines are always at pains to tell us how wonderful the experience of flying is. Flight announcements prior to take-off always end with words such as, *Enjoy your flight,* and, though some airlines have the good grace to say that they "hope" you enjoy it, so many things conspire to render this about as likely as winning the lottery that the words never ring true. After all, how can several hours crushed in a tiny seat inside a metal tube, being dehydrated, watching a cut-down version of a film of which the best review said "dire", and eating what is described as dinner at breakfast time or three in the morning be in any small way pleasurable?

You have a significant choice when you make a flight booking. Will you turn right or left as you enter the plane? Bearing in mind that on long-haul flights you need a mortgage (if you can get one) even to fly economy, and that business class needs a budget like the GNP of a small country, the choice may very well be made for you – by your bank manager. If financially you can run to the upper classes however it certainly helps a tad, but even then, there is one obstacle to a smooth flight that is difficult to control.

What's that?

It is the person who sits next to you.

Think about it. Half the population seem to make unpleasant travelling companions: the overweight, intoxicated, and those with verbal diarrhoea or flatulence; also, insomniacs, fidgets, babies and small unruly children, and many more. Watch the scene in any airport lounge. No one makes goo-goo eyes at babies or pulls faces at other people's children, especially in these days of reducing parental discipline. The sight of them fills us with dread. Me, I just hope some kind of seat selection god exists and pray silently for any obnoxious ankle biter to be at the other end of the plane from me; or, better still, left behind. Perhaps the airlines could clamp down a little: *I am sorry Mrs Stephens, but little Wayne is far too noisy and will have to be checked into the hold.* I once saw a sign in an airport saying, "Parents' Room", maybe it was so that parents could hide away as their children roamed the airport alone wreaking havoc.

Some fellow passengers are bizarre: I once spent 11 hours sitting next to a terrified undertaker on his first flight, unable to stop talking about his grisly profession and the air crash bodies that had passed through his premises – *I charged the full whack even when much of them was missing,* he said – as I wondered where this would lead by the time the flight ended.

Given the number of people travelling these days and the airlines' need only to fly packed flights, guaranteeing that the seat next to you will be empty is well-nigh impossible. On anything but budget airlines, where you need to wear running shoes as you board to ensure getting any space at all, especially for your bag, seats are usually pre-allocated. Tactics that work on a bus say, simply cannot apply. On a bus incidentally, it is no good putting bags down to block the seat beside you, the kind of person you want to discourage will take a perverse pleasure in asking you to move them. Better to pat the seat next to you, drool a little and give people a maniacal smile; no one wants to sit next to an obvious nutter. Nor, back to planes, can you guarantee that a gorgeous, doe-eyed nymphomaniac who unaccountably fancies you to bits and is intent on joining the mile-high club will occupy the seat next to you either. Still less can you guarantee that it will not be occupied by a stressed mother whose fractious two-year old screams without pause and wholly unchecked throughout the entire flight, and who asks you to hold things as she changes nappies right in front of you.

But one man has set out to help with all this.

Following in the footsteps of web sites like Friends Reunited, American Peter Shankman has set up the site airtroductions.com. This allows you to register your personal details alongside details of any flight you plan to take and to enter details too of what kind of person you would like to sit next to you. The success of this is dependent, of course, on someone else who is both on your flight and logs onto the same site actually liking the sound of your details and agreeing to sit next to you. Or indeed on you succeeding in finding someone who suits you. It must make for some odd requests: *Nervous first-time flyer, non-smoker, seeks more experienced neighbour for handholding and maybe more.* Or: *Experienced jet setter seeks to join mile high club with like-minded soul with good stamina and low boredom threshold.* Actually, it is a form of what is now popularly known as networking and the site's proud founder is quoted as saying: "We all fly so much, I thought there must be a better way to use all that time in the air. I have sat next to chief executives, marketing directors and movie stars. The discussions have led to gaining new clients, lots of business and even a date or two."

Personally, for the most part I have rarely if ever sat

next to anyone on an aircraft who did not disturb me in some way or another or bored me silly if we got talking. So, I find the thought of sitting next to some weird web surfing traveller, who not only thinks that this form of travel-companion finding is a neat idea, but who is also actually prepared to pay to register with it (yes, there's a charge!), really very scary. Even the nutter on the bus is not usually that worrying. It did not surprise me that, looking up this site again recently, it seemed to have disappeared.

So, I have resolved to take my chances and have so far declined to log on and add my name to any such list. In any case what would I say? Maybe: *Cynical traveller seeks slim, sober, tongue-tied travel companion wanting to sleep through the entire flight; will supply sleeping pill.* Or: *Is anyone out there booked on my flight, and has a family emergency that will prevent them from travelling? May I have your unoccupied seat next to me please?*

Enough; they are calling my flight. I'll just keep my fingers crossed and pray I'm not seated next to that undertaker again.

I hope this penultimate item, "Are you sitting comfortably?", made you smile. Certainly, if you have done any amount of air travel you can probably identify with it. I must have taken a large number of flights over the years, many on business, and many long-haul; I always carry a notebook and regularly find the experience provides an idea or two to fuel my writing. For example, the undertaker in this piece was all too real. Travel is an area I return to regularly in my writing. I once wrote a regular column for a travel magazine published in Singapore, but sadly it ceased publication. Details of my three books of light-hearted travel writing appear a few pages on.

Afterword

"There are three rules for writing the novel. Unfortunately, no one knows what they are."
             W. Somerset Maugham.

I was bounced into writing a long time ago at a time when I thought it would be the last thing I ever did. My then boss had written a business book that proved very successful. So much so that the publisher wanted more. Rather than set to again himself he asked me (and one or two others in the firm) to write one; told me to do so would describe it better. Though he said it was only a suggestion, he also said I should bear in mind who it was making it! Even so my initial response was to protest – *I can't write a book!* – but to no avail. He asked if I could write a page on the subject (which I knew) so I had to agree that I could do that. He then explained that if I did that and then wrote another page and did that, say, a hundred and fifty more times… I would have a book. This was in the days when, pre-computers, I then had to write the book out by hand, a secretary typed it, I edited it, and this meant more typing and finally a manuscript went to the publisher and the book duly appeared. Now safely long out of print, my rudimentary writing style embarrasses me if I dig it out and have a look back. Nevertheless, it sold well. I went on to write more, and found that, having struggled to find out more about how to write better, I was hooked. Many writers become somewhat obsessive about their craft; I know I get withdrawal symptoms if I don't have some project on the go.

These days I would say that I love writing and all that goes with it, including the contact I have with other writers in various ways: for example, through writing groups I belong to and talks I have given about aspects of the writing process. I also love to encourage others with their writing and have played a small part with a number of people over the years in assisting their journey to publication. One or two people I have even co-authored books with... and managed to do so without falling out!

It has been said that "everyone has a book in them." The majority do not. However, some people love writing or want to give it a try; what is now called life writing, creating a diary-style record of one's life (rather than a full-blown autobiography) is one particular form increasing in popularity, primarily with creating something for family members to read in mind. Others have larger ambitions.

Fiction can be particularly satisfying to write, even if, as the quotation from Somerset Maugham above points up, the process involved is a somewhat mysterious one. The short story form exemplified here provides a straightforward way for anyone to try writing. As I explained in the introduction, the first piece (other than business material) that I had published was a mini saga of a mere fifty words. One can write essays (and rants, which can be fun), stories in many different genres, reminiscences, and more all in a way that is self-contained in two, three, four pages – say from fifty to three/four thousand words. Doing this is manageable, possible and a great deal more straightforward than starting by attempting to write a whole book (though do not let me put you off doing that if that is what you want!). Who knows? You could well find it pleasurable, satisfying and love it, so why not give it a go? If you should do so, then I wish you well. Let me know, maybe I could be your first customer.

Patrick Forsyth. Maldon, Essex.
Contact via: www.patrickforsyth.com

Postscript. *I will leave you with one more short piece, not a story, but something about the writing process, which quotes various examples of miswriting; maybe it is a good thing that mistakes are sometimes made, I love such things when, as here, they make me smile.*

Write right

It has been fun getting this collection of my scribblings together. Any writing involves (at least) three stages. First come the ideas, quite how this happens many writers, including myself regard as something of a mystery. It is not just a mystery it is also not always easy. It was Joyce Grenfell who said, "If I knew where my inspiration came from, I would go there again". Secondly even when inspiration has struck you have to get the words that express your ideas down in a correct, clear, original and pleasing way; something I hope I have succeeded in doing here. However careful one is there is usually not only a need for some revision, editing that also adds or subtracts from the first draft, but also to check for things that slip through. For example, it could just be one inappropriately chosen word or something misspelt or mistyped. Chequing (sic) is vital and must focus on every detail. Once when Oscar Wilde was asked what he had been up to one day, he replied that he had spent the morning reviewing a poem that he had written and had taken out a comma. Then, he added, "In the afternoon I put it back". Every writer knows the feeling.

So, much of the time writers spend, when they are not sharpening their pencils or making yet another cup of tea to avoid writing anything at all, is spent editing, amending, adding or deleting and fine tuning in a variety of ways; perhaps plethora of ways puts it better, or maybe surfeit is a more appropriate word ... no, let's just leave it there. Nearly always something is missed; feel free to let me know if you see something here.

If you doubt that it is true that writing is difficult look around at the evidence, private diaries apart, as most writing is meant to be read much is public and clear for all to see. For instance, there was for a while a notice on Paddington station that said, "Passengers must not leave their luggage unattended at any time or they will be taken away and destroyed". This is not evidence of an execution chamber hidden in the basement below Platform 12, it is evidence of just how difficult writing can be and the blindness that can so easily overcome the writer as they struggle to check things – too often we see what we mean and not what we have actually written down. The station sign just mentioned is only a single sentence. If it is difficult to get that much right, then perhaps writers can be forgiven for struggling to complete an article or certainly a whole book, in which every word needs to be appropriately chosen and deployed.

It can be fun to look around further. Once when I checked in at Sydney airport, I was handed a card asking, "Has anything been put in your luggage without your knowledge?" That's a 'don't know', isn't it? Ilfracombe Council offer, "Free micro-chipping for retired people", not so that such people don't get lost, in fact the service is for their dogs. A university web site asks you to enter a password consisting of, "Between 7 and 8 Characters". Hmmm. In fact, anything to do with figures seems to create particular difficulty. A tyre retailer guarantees that their tyres will not need replacing for, "up to 60,000 miles". Worn out and useless after a hundred miles and wanting a replacement? "Oh no governor, read the guarantee". On the basis stated getting to end of the road before they wear out would mean that their promise has been fulfilled. A sign at a ferry terminal announces,

"Shuttles leave every half hour... on the hour"; this was presumably originated not only by a poor writer, but by someone with a pretty odd clock. A recruitment agency advertisement states, "7.5-ton delivery drivers wanted"; surely not so, they'd never get in the cab. And a sign in a department store says, "Ears pierced while you wait" – which seems to imply that there might be some other way to do it.

Again, all these examples are a way short of an article or book. The wording of instructions seems to pose particular problems. A child's scooter has a note with it saying, "This product is not designed to be used on roads". Fair, and safety conscious enough, but further down the list it reads, "Not designed for off-road use". I hope it's nice to look at in that case; perhaps it's designed to hang on the wall like a picture. A jacket, bought at ASDA, is labelled "Machine washable, dry clean only", and worse, a scarf is labelled, "Dry clean only in cold water".One package offers stern advice – "Warning: potatoes – handle with care" – potatoes? Special explosive potatoes, are they? On the A435 there is a sign saying, "No access to vehicles over 10 tons, except for access" and another which declares enigmatically, "Sign not in use" – but it is!

Perhaps my favourite example of such mistakes is a sign in a hotel in Nottinghamshire. It reads, "In the interests of security bedroom doors must be securely locked before entering or leaving the room". A good trick if you can do it... or evidence of a fifth dimension, perhaps. Again, this is only a single sentence, but it is one written, printed and placed on the inside of 256 rooms all apparently without anyone noticing that it was nonsense.

Now some such errors can be checked automatically. On even the most modest computer a spell checker will tell you not to write the word professor with two f's and one s. It checks this sort of thing for you, but it won't even twitch if you write *cheque* instead of *check* as both are real words. You can even install a program on your computer that will read back to you whatever you write. But the voice it does it in is such a *flat and expressionless monotone without any of the correct emphasis* that this is no panacea for accuracy either.

Enough. This becoming a rather long way of suggesting that the checking process is difficult and apologising for any errors that have slipped through here, which reminds me, I have a computer manual by my desk on the first page of which it says: *This manual has been carefully for any errors.* Oops.

OTHER TITLES BY PATRICK FORSYTH

Novels

Long Overdue
Overdue in so many ways

By his own admission, Philip is living a humdrum life in the Essex coastal town of Maldon. His new boss at the town library is a pain in the neck, making even the job he loves difficult, and he longs for something to kick start him out of what he admits is a bit of a rut. Soon after a new and unexpected friendship begins, he determines to make some changes. Then one day his routine walk to work has him finding a dead body, involved with the police and feeling he must help his new friend by investigating a mystery from years past.

As events following the death carry him along, he forms a surprising alliance to hunt down a missing person. He quickly realises that dialling the emergency services that spring morning is leading to changes that will affect his life, his job and his future as well as having him travel abroad and make some surprisingly impulsive decisions.

"It comes with a real ear for dialogue and a pulse-quickening sense of risk. As for Philip, he is a thoroughly well-rounded protagonist for whom you root from the start." The Good Book Guide

Loose Ends
Her death was only the start of it

Philip's life is back on track, going well and he plans to improve it further. But his tendency to get involved with other peoples' problems remains. A chance encounter in the library leads him towards a psychic incident, and sorting out the loose ends following the death of his neighbour sees him discover a mysterious break-in and make a new friend. Soon he finds that, far from just recommending suitable reading choices to those visiting his library, his influence stretches much further: ultimately having effects on the other side of the world and prompting changes for both himself and others.

A Rather Curious Crime
Curious, very curious

Alice Carter always wanted to be a journalist. Still new to her first job as a junior reporter on a local newspaper she reckons her editor seems to be stuck viewing her as the office dogsbody. Nevertheless, she tackles everything conscientiously while also looking for a new home in the town in which she now lives.

She is learning a lot; however, no one knows more about the ideal costume to wear for a fun run or how many pies it is impressive to eat in a pie eating contest, and she hopes planned visits to the local library and a top executive will prove of more interest than competitive pie eating.

While the routine is getting to Alice, elsewhere someone is laying plans for a criminal act in the town which will mix danger and hope in a curious way – and which is not in any way routine.

Once a thief
From a life at risk... to lives changed forever
Tracy Hines is in a rut, unsure where her future lies but determined to escape a dead-end job in the nether regions of a supermarket. Then a burst of honesty lands her an unusual apprenticeship and sets her on a new and unexpected course. It is one that begins to change her life and holds out a variety of possibilities for the future.

Meantime a thief has his eyes on what he believes is

a particularly good opportunity, albeit one that exposes him to greater risk than usual. When his carefully laid plans do not play out as he hoped a chain of events is set in train that profoundly affects him and others.

Tracy is affected more than most and finds herself surprised, threatened and faced with a puzzle that could change her life still further.

"Once again Patrick gives us charming characters who are in a world of trouble. A twisty plot that has you guessing till the last page" Tony Fisher BBC broadcaster and writer.

Stop press: currently, as I write, a screenplay is being written of this story. It makes an interesting project for me to observe but is perhaps a million miles from seeing it on television... still, I tell myself – you never know! PF

Where there's a will
If it's true – someone dies.

Visiting a prison inmate as a favour to a distant relative, Kathy has an unexpected encounter and forms a new friendship. When a disturbing rumour prompts them to embark on a mission to prevent a tragedy, they find themselves following a frustrating path, one involving the prison authorities, the police and ruthless and illegal measures being taken in the City of London. Though events are regularly punctuated with tea and cake, the two new friends find pursuing matters more complicated than they thought as their resolve is heightened by the repeating thought: "What if it were true?" Seeking to answer the question against the clock brings many consequences and exposes them to more danger than they ever imagined.

"Once again Patrick brings a mixture of intrigue and plot twisting while creating characters you might meet

down the coffee shop." Tony Fisher, BBC broadcaster and writer.

Note: four of the novels are set in my hometown of Maldon.

The travel writing

First class at last!

Fed up with the grisly aspects of travel: the slow queues, the delays, the crowds and the extreme discomfort of flying?The author did something about it – embarking on 12,000 miles of luxury travel from London to Singapore and Bangkok.

Flying first class, staying in Raffles Hotel in Singapore and The Oriental in Bangkok he travelled between them, through three countries along the Malaysian peninsula, on what has been called the best train ride in the world – the Eastern & Oriental train (the Orient Express of the East).

Obviously, reporting on such a first-class experience is hard work (though someone had to do it) – this lively, wry and amusing account highlights what every traveller wants to do: throw the budget out the window and explore a fascinating part of the world in style!

"...lively, witty and wry "Select Books

"...it reminded me of Bryson ..." Neal Asher (bestselling science fiction author of *Gridlinked* and more*).*

Beguiling Burma

Burma (Myanmar to some) is increasingly in the news as some change begins. Ruled for many years by a ruthless, repressive junta, it suffers regular earthquakes and cyclone Nargis left more than a hundred thousand people injured, homeless or dead.

Yet this is a magical place: a country of contrasts with a rambunctious history and a culture that is both awesome and fascinating. Largely on a whim, the author decides to visit Mandalay, the "Golden City" foreseen by ancient Buddhist prophesies. Despite campaigns at the time suggesting no one travelled to Burma (thus supporting the regime) he takes a trip, much of it on the river cruiser *Road to Mandalay* sailing along the famous Ayeyarwady.

He finds people are universally welcoming. Along the way he encounters taxis pulled by oxen; rings the largest bell in the world; learns how to wear a skirt, the difference between a stupa and a pagoda and why fluorescent pink tiles are used in temples.

In this lively and light-hearted account of his journey he watches the best sunset in the world on the plains of Bagan and, as the sun sinks below the horizon silhouetting countless pagodas, concludes that this wonderful country is worthy of everyone's attention, and perhaps help too.

"(Patrick is) a born writer with a clear, transparent style, a great eye, and plenty of wit... miles superior to most of the travel writing I read, and I read lots of it. It's also deeply felt, which is probably the most important thing of all... I was really, really impressed." Timothy Hallinan (bestselling author of the bestselling Poke thrillers set in Southeast Asia).

Smile because it happened

Smile and the world smiles with you; so says the song – but it sometimes seems that we are assailed on all sides by maudlin. So many people we cross paths with are apparently unable to crack a smile. It can get you down and we need an antidote; one such is the land of smiles.

Whether you know Thailand or plan to or just dream of the exotic east, the book will put a smile on your face. One reviewer describes it further:

Even if the "Land of Smiles" still appears to present a few challenges to your average traveller and many more to its own citizens, the author is convinced that Thailand is a happier place than home and that attitude is the key. His affable style and entertaining anecdotes are designed to instil optimism, while stirring real-life stories of resourcefulness and cheerfulness in the face of privations and frustration inspire imitation. Particularly to be recommended for visitors to Thailand, this may indeed cure melancholy, if only by pointing out that life back in Blighty is relatively cushy and that smiles cost nothing. The Good Book Guide

Printed in Great Britain
by Amazon